COLD TERROR

A COLD HARBOR NOVEL - BOOK ONE
(NOVELLA)

SUSAN SLEEMAN

EDGE OF YOUR SEAT BOOKS, INC.

Published by Edge of Your Seat Books, Inc.

Contact the publisher at contact@edgeofyourseatbooks.com

Copyright © 2017 by Susan Sleeman

Cover design by Kelly A. Martin of KAM Design

All rights reserved. Without limiting the rights under copyright reserved above, no part of this book may be reproduced in any form or by any electronic or mechanical means, including information storage and retrieval systems, without permission in writing from the publisher, except by a reviewer, who may quote brief passages in a review.

This book is a work of fiction. Characters, names, places, and incidents in this novel are either products of the imagination or are used fictitiously. Any resemblance to real people, either living or dead, to events, businesses, or locales is entirely coincidental.

1

"Murder and vacation *do not* go together!"

Forensic artist Hannah Perry held her phone away from her ear to keep her friend Rachel's voice from breaking her eardrum. "Vacation or not, I had to agree to do the reconstruction."

"Had to, no. Wanted to, yes."

"You don't understand. Jane Doe needs a name. She needs me." Hannah waited for Rachel to sigh, but she didn't, and her long silence was even worse.

"I don't pretend to understand how it feels to have a sister abducted and never come home," she finally said. "To be driven every day to help others in similar situations. But I do understand the stress you've been under since Nick died, and you need a break."

Rachel was right. Of course, she was. As a professional counselor, she'd been instrumental in helping Hannah get through the loss of her husband and always knew when Hannah had reached the breaking point. In fact, this vacation was her idea. But...

Hannah's gaze drifted to the woman's unidentified skull perched on the small dining table in the quaint rental cottage. What had this woman looked like? Was she blond, brunette, or maybe she even had blazing red hair like Hannah's. Either way, Jane Doe deserved to be identified. How could Hannah say no to completing a facial reconstruction that might very well lead to the woman's identity and bring closure to her family?

"If you won't think of your own mental health, then think of David," Rachel continued. "He's a little boy, and this is his last vacation before school starts. He needs his mother to be present for him."

"I *am* present," Hannah snapped with more force than necessary. "I only work on the reconstruction at night."

"But I'll bet you think about it during the day."

"Okay, fine, maybe I do, but the investigation has stalled, and Jane has no one else."

Poor Jane. Her body had been discovered in a gravel pit near where Hannah was vacationing on the Oregon coast. She'd barely picked up the keys for the cottage when news spread through town about her career. Then the sheriff had shown up on her doorstep the second morning and pled with her to do a facial reconstruction. After her own sister had been abducted when they were teenagers, Hannah had never been able to refuse anyone needing her help. After all, that was the reason she'd become a forensic artist.

"I appreciate your concern, Rach, but I can't afford to waste time arguing." Hannah smoothed the clay over Jane's high cheekbone to fill in her muscles and stood back to appraise her work.

One more press of her finger above the cheekbone. Yes, that was it. Perfect. The underlying facial structure was perfect.

She let her hand fall and was suddenly aware that Rachel had been talking, but Hannah's work had taken over and she had no idea what Rachel had said.

"You've gone back to the skull, haven't you?" Rachel asked.

"Sorry."

"I guess there's nothing I can say that will convince you to relax and enjoy that fabulous secluded cottage."

"I promise not to think about Jane during the day, but the nights belong to her."

"That's something I guess. Text me a few pictures of you and David having fun."

"You just want proof that I'm following through."

"You know it." Rachel chuckled.

Hannah laughed, and after ending the call, she stretched her arms toward the ceiling covered in white shiplap. She desperately wanted Jane to be identified, but Hannah needed a short break before starting on the tissue depth markers. She had a bad habit of hunching over the table resulting in headaches if she didn't stretch and get some fresh air.

She crossed over the rough-hewn floors to the front porch only big enough for the two chairs bolted in place. Wind howled from the ocean, battering her body back against the cottage, but the cool air was refreshing. She braced her feet against the late summer storm and stared into the dusky sky. Choppy waves crashed into the rock-lined coast, the spray misting the air. Offshore, a small fishing boat bounced on rough waves, rising and falling with the surf stirred up by an impending storm.

"Foolish to be out in this kind of weather," she muttered as she stepped back inside, forced the door closed, then locked it. She'd been a competitive college rower and had continued rowing for exercise, but even she wouldn't try to navigate such choppy waters, much less in the fading light.

Back at the table, she settled headphones over her ears to tune out the wind. The sultry jazz tones of Garfunkel's "I

Only Have Eyes for You" emptied her mind, and she started to cut long tubular erasers.

The song ended, and before the next one started, she heard the floor creak. If she was home in her condo with solid concrete floors, she would jump, but not here. The cottage was set on stilts due to flooding, and it groaned and moaned with even a light wind. Tonight it was positively swaying. Besides, no one else inhabited the island, which was precisely why she'd chosen the secluded location.

The next song spilled through the headphones, and she hummed along as she finished slicing differing-length markers. Once cut, she would attach them to the skull in twenty-one predefined locations to help determine the right depth for the clay. She glanced at her chart for a European female, and using her measurements, she started affixing the markers to the skull.

She leaned closer. An unexpected movement to her side caught her attention. She turned to look. Before she could make out the object, an arm shot around her neck and jerked back, pulling her against a hard body.

A scream came to her lips, but the paralyzing hold cut off her oxygen.

"You thought I wouldn't find out." The man's deep baritone came from behind, anger vibrating through his words. "I won't let you destroy me."

"Help!" she managed to squeak out as she clawed at his forearm. Her fingernails gained purchase, drawing blood.

He muttered a string of curses. A gloved hand slammed into her temple, and pain razored into her skull. Nausea swam through her stomach. Blackness threatened.

She blinked hard. Blinked again.

The darkness was winning. Drawing, pulling her toward the black void.

No! Don't give in. David lost his dad. He needs you.

4

She forced her eyes open. Kept clawing at the arm and looked over the table for something—anything to fight him off.

The needle tool. She grabbed it and plunged the steel into his arm. Hit bone. Jerked it out. Blood spurted freely.

Curses spewed from his mouth, and his arm loosened. She stabbed again.

Once. Twice. Three times.

He howled and let her go.

Gasping for breath, she snatched up her ball peen hammer from the table. Spun and swung it hard. The steel slammed into his head covered by a ski mask. He went down like a boxer connecting with a hard punch.

Mind racing, Hannah ripped off her headphones and sucked in air. Her throat was sore, the skin tender and bruised, but she couldn't focus on the pain. She had to act.

The man lay unmoving, but still the threat emanated from him.

What should she do? Stay here and call for help? Go outside in the brewing storm?

She couldn't use her phone. Even if she could get a signal, which was iffy, it would take too long for anyone to arrive in the raging storm. Remaining in the cottage was certain death, right? Maybe if she had something to tie him up with and buy time, but what?

Think, Hannah, think!

She shot a look around. Spotted her phone cord. A lamp cord. They wouldn't make a firm knot to hold him. She had to leave, but how? The ocean was probable death, too.

Oh my gosh, David.

What about David? She had to save him.

Run. Now.

Yes, run. She grabbed her jacket. Raced to his small bedroom and saw her precious five-year-old son asleep on his stomach. Fist tucked under his chin. Rump up in the air. Dreaming of wonderful things, not the nightmare in the other room.

Please help us! Help me to take him on this dangerous journey.

"Wake up, David." She shook his shoulder. Gently at first. He didn't stir. "Now, Son!" She shook harder until his powder-blue eyes opened, and he blinked, his soft red hair stuck to his forehead.

"We have to leave now." She lifted him into her arms and wrapped him in the quilt, covering his eyes from seeing the monster on the floor, but her son had gone back to sleep. *Perfect.*

She hurried for the door. Found her attacker stirring.

No! She'd spent too much time thinking and now he was awake.

She jerked open the door. The wind buffeted her. She fought hard and trudged onto the tiny porch. Down the stairs. Across the yard and over the boat ramp's worn boards. Her small rowboat and her attacker's boat bobbed on opposite sides of the dock.

Footsteps sounded from the porch.

She risked a glance back. Saw the man. Tall. Foreboding. Filling the open doorway. Interior lights spilling around him. He shook his head as if trying to clear his brain.

She wouldn't be here when he did.

She settled her sleeping son in the small rowboat, then untied her attacker's boat and set it adrift.

His footsteps barreled down the steps, but a limp seemed to slow him down.

Hurry! Hurry!

She got to her feet. Crossed the dock and dropped down into her boat. With an oar, she gave a solid push away from the dock just as the attacker reached the end. She plunged her oars in the water, and thankful for her rowing experience, she propelled the boat forward.

The wind howled over the bow, water spit and sprayed in her face, but she managed to move far enough away from the attacker so he couldn't leap into her boat. He stood on the dock, raising his fist and shaking it.

"This isn't over," he shouted into the wind.

She memorized the voice so if she ever heard it again she could call him out, then turned her attention to escaping.

Heavy chop rocked the boat while waves crashed over the hull and water settled in the bottom. At this rate, they'd soon fill with water and sink. She couldn't let that happen. She had to move.

Faster. Faster.

Adrenaline fueled her arms. When the attacker was no longer visible, she tied a life jacket securely on David and turned the boat toward shore. She glanced behind her to see if the man was in sight.

Forget him. Move.

A large wave took them high and crashed them down hard.

"Mommy." David's eyes were huge. "Why are we here?"

"I need you to stay down, Son."

"But—"

"No buts. Do as I say!" The words came out harsher than she'd like, but she had no time to convince him to listen.

"We're almost there," she said, softer now as the lights of Cold Harbor appeared ahead. Beckoning her. "Hold on, Son!"

They rose on the surf again. Plummeted down. Water nipped her calves, and she paused in her rhythm to look at the bottom of the boat. A foot of water had settled inside, and the boat rode dangerously low.

She had to hurry. *Move.* She started rowing in long, even pushes, riding the ocean swells, each one adding to the pool of water. A sudden gust of wind caught the boat's bow, turning them from shore.

She frantically rowed trying to turn them around. Sideways now, a monstrous wave rolled toward them.

They were going to capsize.

No!

She let go of the oars to dive for David. She lifted him into her arms.

The water hit like a tidal wave.

The boat swirled. Churned. Turned. Lifted. Crashed down, wrenching David from her arms.

"David!" she screamed, panic overwhelming her as the water washed over her head and took her into the deadly depths.

Gage Blackwell paused on the dune and strained his eyes for a better view of the shoreline. Had he really seen the boat? The one that a twenty-foot wave just tossed into the air?

Yes, there it was again, slamming into a boulder and ejecting two people into the frigid ocean. One he guessed was an adult. The other small enough to be a child.

What kind of fool took a rowboat out on a night like this, much less brought a child with them? Didn't matter. They needed his help, even if it was dangerous for anyone to enter the angry waves.

He raced down the dune, the sand fighting to take him down, but he powered on, counting on years of running on the beach and years of Navy SEAL training to see him through.

Ahead, he saw the pair. A female and a child. She was clutching the child in her arms and floundering. She suddenly shoved the child up over a crashing wave and disappeared.

"Mommy!" the boy screamed as he clawed through the foam to remain upright. "Mommy!"

Gage reached the shoreline and shed his jacket and shoes. He barreled into the icy water, grabbed the boy, and sloshed through the currents, carrying him to safety. He wrapped the drenched child in his jacket, then set him on the sand. The boy shivered, his hair dripping and freckled face pale, but he didn't seem hurt in any way. Gage could now see the child was five, maybe six, the same age his Mia had been when she'd nearly died.

No. Don't go there.

"My mommy," the little voice said, wrenching Gage's heart.

He squinted at the surf, waiting for the woman to come back up. She did. Briefly. Gasping. Fighting.

He dug out his phone. "Do you know how to call 911?"

The boy nodded, teeth chattering.

"Then stay here and call." Gage handed his phone to the child and plunged back into the frothy waves. The sixty-degree surge of water hit him like an ice bath, but his SEAL training taught him to ignore it, and he pushed toward the spot where the woman went down. He'd acclimated his body to the cold over the years and could survive longer, but the water temperature was life threatening to her if he didn't get to her soon.

She popped up just ahead, arms flailing, her head barely breaking the water.

"Hold on. I'm coming," he called out, his mouth filling with salty liquid.

"Help," she got out before a wave crashed over her head.

9

He started to swing his arms against the tide, his right arm nearly worthless in the current. *Right.* It didn't work well anymore. Had taken him out of the SEALs. Gave him a new life. This life.

His body slid back in the cresting wave. *No. No.* He had to forget about the pain. The weakness. She needed him. A woman needed him. He wouldn't fail her.

He gulped in air and put his face in the shadowy water. When he reached the spot where she'd gone down, he dove in. Deep. To the bottom. Felt through the murkiness. Touched fabric. Grabbed it and jerked her up, then swam to the surface.

The petite woman broke the water. She coughed and gagged but didn't fight him. From behind, he got his good arm around her chest to ensure he didn't lose her in the pummeling waves and paddled with his gimpy arm. Something wet and sticky found his face. Not water, but blood. He knew the feel. The smell from his military days. She'd likely hit her head on a boulder or the boat. Not only was she at risk for hypothermia if he didn't get her out of the water soon, but the head injury put her in even more danger.

He tried to pick up his pace, but his arm slowed them down.

"David?" He heard her ask, and he assumed she meant the boy.

"On shore...he's fine," Gage replied, though he had no idea if the child really was okay.

He wanted to reassure the woman she would be fine, but he had no breath left to talk. He'd once been so able-bodied and could have brought this woman in easily. But since the accident, he'd had to work twice as hard with his arm to accomplish half as much.

"Mommy," the boy's shriek broke through the roar of the storm. "I called 911. They're coming!"

The woman sagged against Gage, the little fight she'd had evaporating—the protector was gone, now that her son was safe. Gage couldn't relax. Not yet. He estimated she'd been in the water for less than fifteen minutes, but still cold shock had likely caused a loss of breathing control, and she would become progressively weaker. Still, it took at least thirty minutes for hypothermia to set in for average adults, even in freezing water. Thankfully, it hadn't been that long yet and the water wasn't freezing.

He paddled the last few yards, then found his footing in the chest-deep water. After using the last of his strength to push through the current, he clambered to safety and collapsed on the sand, still holding her. He maneuvered her limp body carefully, pulled soggy red hair aside, and caught his first look at her face in the moonlight.

Shock traveled through his system, and he blinked hard to look again.

"Hannah?" he asked, but her eyes were closed and she didn't respond.

Could it really be her, back in his life again after so many years?

Tons of questions followed, but the sight of her wounded temple grabbed his attention. He wished he had a first aid kit. He needed to disinfect the wound and immediately warm her body until the medics arrived. Air temps weren't much higher than the water, and if he didn't slow her heat loss, she'd be headed for hypothermia.

David came stumbling toward them, his large blue eyes so much like Hannah's.

"Hey, buddy, let's put my jacket around your mother." Gage wrapped Hannah snugly in his large coat and tucked David under his arm for warmth.

"Mommy. Wake up, Mommy." David took her limp hand

2
———

Strong arms held her, that much Hannah knew. Anything else? Maybe the cold—the bone-shattering, violent shivering until your body seized with it—cold that enveloped her entire being. She vaguely heard sirens in the distance. For her? Was she hurt?

Think. What happened? The attack. The boat.

David! No—David.

She forced her lids open to find intense eyes burrowing into hers. A man was holding her. She had a sense of homecoming but couldn't place why. He was dark-haired and rugged with a shadow of whiskers covering his wide jaw, his eyes a dark slate-blue. His nose was large and crooked with a bump at the top as if it had been broken. Something about him said safety. Security—dependability—and she had an urge to run a finger over the bump, but her arms felt like heavy weights held them down.

"Welcome back." His full lips split in a smile as sirens sounded in the distance.

Yes, she knew him, but her foggy brain wouldn't reveal how.

"Mommy," she heard David say, and suddenly his face filled her vision.

"Mommy," he said again, this time on a breathy sigh. "You woke up."

"Of course I did." She dug deep for the strength to smile, then frowned over the blue tint to his lips and his shivering body. "You're cold."

"Gage is keeping us warm."

"Gage?" She shifted and drank in the face she never expected to see again. "Gage? Is it really you?"

"Yes."

"He pulled us out of the water," David said solemnly. "He's a hero, and I called the ambulance."

"You're the real hero." Gage smiled at David. "The medics are almost here, thanks to you for being brave and making the call."

Gage. They hadn't seen each other in—what?—almost ten years, but they'd been oh-so-in-love back then. And now? He kept smiling at David and being so sweet to her son. Maybe he had children of his own. She glanced at his ring finger but found it empty. She'd heard he'd married, but then he'd left the SEAL team her husband had belonged to, and she'd lost track of him.

The siren grew louder, and she would have wiggled out of his arms, but her body wouldn't respond. She felt safe and secure, despite the cold and pain in her head.

A big sigh of relief welled up inside. Safe. Yes, safe.

No, wait! She wasn't safe after the assault in the cottage, her throat likely bearing the marks from the man's deathly grip. If not for her tools, she'd be dead. And David...

A shudder raked over her body. *No.* She wouldn't go there.

"I'm sorry about the cold," Gage said, shivering himself. "I don't have anything but my jacket to keep you warm."

"Thank you for sharing it." She rested against his solid chest, his powerful long legs holding her the same way he'd done many times. Until he didn't. Until he'd left her behind without a glance. The familiar pain settled into her heart, but she couldn't think about that now. She had to think about getting herself and David to safety.

"How are you doing?" he asked. "Can you stop shivering?"

She tried and succeeded. "Yes."

"Good. So can David."

She cast Gage a questioning look.

"It means your body temps may have lowered due to the cold, but any hypothermia you might be experiencing is mild. The medics will soon be here, and everything will be fine."

She sighed out a breath, but her attention went to flashing red lights and the siren whirling close. Ambulance or police?

"Did you call the police?" she asked.

"No. Should I have?"

David's eyes widened, his interest clearly piqued. She wouldn't talk about the attacker in front of him, so she shook her head until a swirling wave of dizziness stopped her.

"What are you doing in town?" Gage asked. "And out in a boat in this weather?"

"Just visiting...at Heavenly Hideaway."

He gaped at her for a moment. "Then you're the one doing the—"

"Reconstruction," she burst in and gave him a pointed look to silence him before David learned about Jane Doe.

A clipped nod told her he understood.

"How did you know?" she asked.

"Small town. We not only know everyone, but we know what they're doing most of the time, too."

"Oh, right." This had to be how her attacker discovered she was working on Jane's skull and where to find her.

"And why in the boat?" he asked.

She still wouldn't talk about the attack, so she turned her head toward the strobing red lights settling in one location. Two medics soon crested the dune, a tall blond male and petite woman with jet-black hair. Medic bags were slung over their shoulders as they trudged across the sand carrying a backboard holding blankets.

The male arrived first, surprise lighting his face. "Gage, that you?"

"Hey, Terry. Glad you got here so fast."

After removing Gage's coat, Terry immediately wrapped Hannah in blankets, covering her from head to toe but leaving one arm out. Gage put his coat back on and reached out for her. She settled back in his arms and watched the other medic wrap David in a large blanket and hold him close.

"I'm Vicki," she said. "What's your name?"

"David."

Vicki continued to talk to him, but her son's gaze remained fixed on Gage as he told the medics how he'd witnessed the boat capsize and his quick rescue.

"I think I got them out of the water in time," Gage added. "Both of them can voluntarily stop shivering, and my SEAL training tells me that's a good sign."

Terry nodded and pressed his fingers against Hannah's wrist. "Can you count backwards from one hundred?"

She had no idea why, but she started counting.

"Good," Terry said, stopping her at eighty-five. "You're coherent, your pulse is strong, and you're shivering. All of that suggests your hypothermia—if any—is mild. Same for your son." He took his stethoscope from around his neck. "You're both very lucky. No better place to capsize than with a former SEAL standing by."

"Former?" She looked up at Gage as Terry listened to her chest. "You left your team?"

"Yes."

She couldn't miss the longing in his tone. Her husband had been a SEAL, and she knew all about their creed and dedication to the job. Never had she met more trustworthy and honorable men. Nothing could have taken Nick away from his job. Nothing. Until he died. Gage had once felt the same way. So why had he quit the team?

"Not just a SEAL." Terry hung his stethoscope around his neck. "But a hero many times over."

"I'm a hero today," David piped up. "Gage said so."

"If Gage says so, then it must be true." Terry grinned at David, then focused back on Hannah.

"Well, little hero," Vicki said. "We need to get you and your mom into the ambulance and on the way to the hospital where they'll have nice warm blankets for you."

David's bravado evaporated, and he nibbled on his lower lip that was still a dark shade of blue. She hated seeing her son distressed over the medic's care. Since Nick died, David had an unreasonable fear of medical professionals.

"It's okay, David." Gage smiled. "Vicki is my friend, and I promise she won't hurt you. Besides, heroes have to be brave, right?"

David's focus remained fixed on Gage for a moment, then he nodded. "I'm brave."

Terry strapped Hannah on the board. "You'll need stitches, and I wouldn't be surprised if you have a concussion."

David's eyes went wide again. "Are you going to die like Dad?"

"No, of course not."

"But he had a 'cussion."

"No, he...sweetie, I'll be fine." She forced a smile, but her heart sank at the reminder of Nick's fall from a towering cliff and internal injuries that he couldn't recover from.

"We need to get moving, Ms. Perry." Terry circled his stethoscope around his neck. "And maybe on the way you can tell me about the bruising—"

"Later," she interrupted before David heard about the injuries to her neck.

Terry raised a brow, but thankfully he got the hint and didn't ask additional questions. She wanted her attacker caught, but protecting David came first. She'd get the police in on this as soon as possible, and then she had to figure out what to do after she was discharged from the ER because her attacker promised this wasn't over.

His hate-filled eyes roving over her, threatening and burning with rage flashed into her mind. Fear followed. She had to get well and get out of town so this maniac didn't come anywhere near David again.

Vicki set David down and freed his feet so he could walk, then the medics picked up her board. She glanced at Gage. "You should get out of those wet clothes and indoors ASAP."

"Trust me. I've been far colder in my SEAL career." He looked at Hannah. "Best of luck to you two."

What? He wasn't coming with them?

Of course he wasn't. He'd left her once before when they were in love. Why should she expect he'd want to stay with her now? She should close her eyes. Forget about him and let him go, but she had David's safety to think about. They needed Gage's protection until she could talk to the police and find someone else to keep them safe.

She grabbed his forearm. "Come with us."

His mouth opened in surprise.

"Please," she added for David's sake.

"I don't know. I—"

"Please," David's little voice echoed.

Gage looked at David, a fond look claiming his face. He gave a quick nod. "Can I catch a ride in the front, Vicki?"

"You got it." She gave him a wide smile.

"Thank you." Hannah squeezed his arm, and the realization of what she'd done hit her hard.

She had asked the man she'd once thought she'd marry, before he bailed on her, to stay by her side. Such a foolish action couldn't be a good thing. Not a good thing at all.

Hannah.

Gage had rescued Hannah of all people, now here he was in an ambulance with her riding in the back. She hadn't changed. She still had that fragile beauty with strength riding underneath. A powerful combination and he was instantly drawn to her again.

Man, he'd once loved her, but she deserved someone who could commit to a long-term relationship. That wasn't him. Not then. Not with all the junk he was dealing with. So he'd had to leave and he'd hurt her. Big time.

And then she'd married one of Gage's former SEAL team members. Gage remembered the day he'd heard about it. Hurt like crazy, but Nick was a good guy. Then sadly, Nick had died a couple of years ago. Gage had wanted to go to the funeral, but that would have been awkward for Hannah. Still, as Gage battled through losing his own spouse, he sometimes wondered how she was doing with her loss and with raising their son.

Now Gage could find out, he supposed. Who knew?

Maybe God had put them together again so he could apologize after all these years. Maybe help her cope, too. He'd sure like the chance.

Vicki pulled the rig under the ER canopy. He opened his door but his palms started to sweat, and he froze in place. He hated hospitals. Had since he was a kid with pneumonia and later when his appendix burst. Then he'd suffered too many injuries to count as a SEAL. And if that wasn't enough, his daughter nearly died in this hospital and was left dealing with the life-altering effects of a traumatic brain injury. His wife sank into a coma here, too, before a transfer to a long-term care center where she'd passed away.

"You coming, Gage?" Vicki asked from outside the vehicle. He'd been so lost in thought he hadn't even heard her approach his door.

He swallowed hard and followed her toward the back of the ambulance where David, still wrapped in a blanket, bounded down while holding Terry's hand. Mia would never be a regular kid like David—thinking, processing, and speaking without difficulties. Sure, she'd improved over time and would still likely continue to improve, but she'd never be so-called "normal" again.

Terry and Vicki unloaded Hannah's gurney, and then Vicki took David's hand to lead him toward the ER doors.

Gage started forward when Hannah's hand came up and wrapped around his arm to pull him close. "I need to talk to you where David can't overhear us."

"Okay." He had no idea what was putting the fear in her incredible blue eyes and why her chin quivered. Maybe this was about their past, and she didn't want her son to know they'd once dated. "I'm sure David will be seen in a separate room from you. If not, once we get inside I'll ask Vicki to sit with him to give us a moment."

She nodded and released his arm while Terry wheeled

her inside. As Gage suspected, the charge nurse directed Terry to take Hannah and David to different rooms. Gage followed Hannah's gurney down the hall where Maggie Turner, a tall slender nurse, waited.

Hannah introduced herself to Maggie then glanced at Gage. "You'll have to excuse us, Gage. Hannah has to get out of her wet clothes. You should, too."

"I will." Knowing Hannah was in good hands with Maggie, he went down the hall to check on David.

When Gage opened the door, he found the boy crying in his bed, a nurse Gage didn't know offering comfort. Gage hated seeing the kid go through this trauma. It was bad enough that he nearly drowned in the stormy ocean, but it seemed as if he equated his injuries with losing his dad. Poor kid. Maybe Gage could help.

"Gage!" David's eyes brightened.

"Hey buddy. How you doing?"

He frowned and held out his arm. "They put a big needle in me."

Gage gave a commiserating nod. "Like I said, heroes have to be tough."

"I'm trying, but mom...I..." Tears glistened in his eyes, and he lowered his head as if ashamed of crying.

Gage crossed over to him. "Listen, buddy. It's okay if you feel like crying. Heroes cry, too. Especially when they're worried about their mothers."

His head popped up. "Really?"

"Really. But the thing is, you don't have to be worried about your mom. She's gonna be okay."

"Honest?"

"Honest," Gage answered and hoped he was right. "Why don't I arrange for you to go see her?"

"Yes!"

Gage patted the boy's hand then returned to Hannah's

room to get permission to bring David in. The door was cracked open so he figured it was safe to enter. Hannah was alone and buried under blankets with one arm out, an IV inserted near her wrist.

She looked up at him with tortured eyes. "Good, we're alone and we can talk now. I was attacked at the cottage. That's how I got the bruises on my neck and why we had to flee in the storm." She lowered the blanket to reveal harsh slashes of purple ringing her delicate neck.

A curse came to Gage's lips, but he squelched it and clenched his hands to control the anger. "Why didn't you say something sooner?"

"David was sleeping when the man attacked, so he doesn't know about it. And I don't want him to."

"How did you get away from the attacker?"

"I hit him over the head with a hammer, grabbed David, and jumped in the boat."

He hated that she'd been through something so horrific. He couldn't even form a word to respond, so he gently tucked the blanket under her chin while he got his emotions under control.

She'd been on a secluded island, miles from the mainland, with no way to escape except in a boat. She'd had to take the life-threatening risk of going out in the storm—with her little boy—or die a certain death at the hands of her attacker. She was likely still terrified, and yet, she was still going. Took a courageous woman to handle such terror. He'd always known she was a strong person, but he was impressed at how deep her strength went.

He would do whatever he could to help her. "I'll call the sheriff."

"Yes, please, but be discreet. David can't know." She met his gaze and held it. "Promise me that. He lost his dad, and he can't think something bad might happen to me, too."

"I heard about Nick's passing. I'm sorry for your loss."

"Thank you, but about the sheriff..." She'd always had a single focus, and that hadn't changed either.

"I'll call him while the doc checks you out."

"Sheriff Blake Jenkins?"

Gage nodded. "I forgot, you must know him from the reconstruction."

"Yes, David knows I'm doing a project for Blake, but not what. I only work on it after David goes to bed. I don't want him to know about the project *or* the attack."

"I have a child, too, so I understand, and I'm sure Blake will as well."

She blinked a few times as if processing the news that he was a father. "Please come back so I know you talked to him. Please."

He nodded.

"Thank you." She sighed out a long breath like she was deflating.

Her pain split his heart. He couldn't just stand there and do nothing. A simple squeeze of her hand was okay, wasn't it? He took a step forward, but the doctor, a short male in blue scrubs, entered the room with Maggie, preempting him. Probably a good thing. A touch from him might very well add to her distress.

"If you'll excuse us, Gage," Maggie said.

He nodded but kept his focus on Hannah. "Before I go, you should know I checked on David. He's hanging in there, but he wants to see you."

"I can make that happen," Maggie offered.

Gage nodded his thanks and left to make his call before he succumbed to Hannah's tortured gaze and rethought his plan to take her hand. He looked around the busy space, trying to find a spot where he could keep an eye on both Hannah's and David's rooms. He found a corner out of the way and dug out his phone that he'd retrieved from David. Gage dialed his high school football buddy, Blake Jenkins, the elected county sheriff for the past six years. He'd captained a strong team in high school and was a well-respected sheriff now.

When he answered, Gage kept his voice down and recounted the little he knew about Hannah's attack. After Blake promised to arrive soon, Gage came to his feet to wait for the doctor to finish his exam. Seemed like hours before he stepped out with Maggie. The pair immediately entered into a hushed conversation sending Gage's concern skyrocketing. Maybe he shouldn't have told David that she would be okay.

Gage hurried to her open door and peeked into the room. The lights were dimmed above her bed, likely due to the head injury. Still, her eyes were clear as they met his. He approached her bed, but her sudden tentative expression slowed his feet.

"Did you reach the sheriff?" she asked.

He nodded when what he wanted to do was ask if she was seriously hurt. For her sake, he needed to cool his worry and wait for her to volunteer the information. And even though he wanted to ask for additional details about the attack, he'd wait until Blake arrived to keep her from having to tell the story twice.

"Blake's on his way." He made sure to smile. "He knows not to speak in front of David."

"Thank you." She frowned.

He'd expected a smile in return. "What is it?"

"I don't have hypothermia, which is a good thing, but the doctor ordered an MRI for the head injury. Depending on what they find, I may have to stay overnight." Tears glistened in her eyes, and she shifted to track Maggie as she stepped back into the room.

"David will be here soon," she said, then met Gage's gaze with a stern look. "I see you didn't take my advice and get changed. I'll grab some scrubs after I get Hannah ready for transport for her MRI."

Hannah's focus changed to Gage. "If I have to spend the night, what am I going to do with David? I don't know anyone in Cold Harbor."

"I can take care of him," Gage said before thinking about it.

A look of pure horror crossed Hannah's face. "You? No. No."

With Blake on the way, she'd likely realized she didn't want Gage to hang around any longer. He deserved her response, but man, it hurt.

"I could call my friend Rachel to come from Portland," she added.

"Why do that when you couldn't ask for anyone better than Gage to watch your son?" Maggie unhooked a lead wire. "He spoils his daughter rotten."

Hannah's mouth opened and closed as if searching for how to respond.

"I can arrange for a bed for David in your room," Maggie offered. "And to make sure you get your rest, Gage can spend the night to keep an eye on David."

"Sure," Gage said, but he doubted Hannah would agree.

"But your daughter and wife," she protested. "They must need you."

He wasn't going to let her use that as an excuse. If she didn't want him around, she would have to come right out and tell him. "My wife passed away three years ago, and I have a live-in nanny who will keep an eye on Mia."

Hannah nibbled on her lip, her eyes narrowed.

"Look." Maggie hooked the IV bag on the edge of the bed. "You can trust Gage. He's the best."

25

Hannah's eyes narrowed even more, and Maggie looked confused.

No confusion for Gage. He got it. He could read Hannah's mind without any trouble. He'd flaked on her before, so why should she trust him now?

3

Gage left, and Hannah ignored Maggie bustling about and reflected on the doctor's diagnosis.

"You have a small bleed on your brain," he'd said. "We'll need to keep you in the hospital so neurosurgery can check on you throughout the night."

The diagnosis she could handle, but a night spent with Gage in her room? With the man who'd been unable to commit to her—worse yet, had taken off instead of committing? How did she handle that? Handle him?

On the one hand, she was glad for his protection. On the other, she'd spent the last few years purposely not depending on a man, and in only a few hours, she'd come to totally depend on Gage.

She sighed and closed her eyes.

Why, God? What's Your plan here?

She sounded like a broken record, repeating the same question since Nick's death. He'd gone hiking. Climbing. Alone. She'd warned him to take a buddy along. But no. He was a SEAL. He didn't need anyone's help to make a simple climb. That was how he'd approached everything in life. He didn't need anyone but his team. And that included her. His attitude had severed all trust and hindered the communication in their marriage.

And now, here she was relying on another man who had similar tendencies. Ironic?

Not funny.

But then, not much had been funny in her life of late. Trying to make a living to support David and still stay home with him for the last two years had been a challenge. Sure, they had Nick's life insurance, but she'd only dipped into that for emergencies and tried to save the rest for David's college fund. He'd start kindergarten after Labor Day and that would make it easier for her to work, but freelancing for all the law enforcement agencies in the Portland area didn't provide steady income or benefits to supplement the meager ones she received from the navy.

At least the doctor hadn't found any issues with David, and he was being released. She didn't know what she'd do if he'd suffered any permanent damage.

She heard the door creak and flashed open her eyes to find Gage entering with Sheriff Blake Jenkins. Gage still wore his soggy running pants and long-sleeved knit shirt that stretched tautly across a muscled chest and arms.

How she'd once loved having those powerful arms wrapped around her. Who was she kidding? She'd liked being in his arms at the beach, too.

He gave her a quizzical look, and she realized she'd been staring. She shifted her attention to Blake who was just over six feet tall, muscular, and fit like Gage. Blake wore a button-down shirt with a leather jacket and jeans. In the event that David entered the room, Hannah was thankful the sheriff had arrived in street clothes.

He stepped over to the bed and offered a kind smile. "You've had quite a night."

Hannah didn't know what to say, so she started to nod, but stopped when a dagger of pain pierced her skull. "I have."

"I saw them readying David for release, so I'll get right to it before they bring him to you." Blake took out a small notepad and pen then pulled up a chair. "When you're ready, go ahead and tell me about the attack."

Hannah took a few deep breaths and let the memories she'd been stifling play out in her mind. "I was working on the reconstruction. My back was to the door. I like to listen to music when I work and had my headphones on. I was totally focused on the project. In between songs, I heard the floor creak but didn't think anything of it as that cottage makes noises. In hindsight, it must have been my attacker creeping up on me."

"Was the door locked?" Blake asked.

"Yes. I have no idea how he got in."

"I dispatched a deputy to the cottage, and hopefully we'll figure that out."

"I assume the creep is long gone."

Blake nodded. "He must have had a boat—did you see it?"

"Yes, it was a small aluminum fishing boat with bright blue oars, but I set it adrift. Maybe he swam for it."

"Or he drowned," Gage said.

"Is it wrong to say I hope so?" She couldn't believe she'd just wished someone had died. "I know it's wrong of me to want anyone to die, but I'll bet he survived. He was crazy strong and could probably figure out a way to stay alive."

Blake frowned. "I have deputies patrolling the waterfront. If he landed and ditched a boat, they'll find it."

"FYI, if you're hoping to find DNA or prints on the boat you should know he wore latex gloves."

"DNA and prints?" Blake smiled. "Your work has obviously taught you about investigations."

She nodded but couldn't smile with him.

"And the attack itself?" Gage asked. "You said he snuck up behind you."

"He clamped an arm around my neck and squeezed." Careful not to disturb her IV, she wrapped her arms around her stomach. She was looking for comfort and protection, and she hoped self-soothing like this would keep her from seeking that comfort from Gage.

"I was nearly blacking out when I got my hands on my needle tool," she continued. "It's exactly like it sounds. I stabbed his arm until he let go. I also have a hammer in my tool kit so I grabbed that and slammed it into his skull. He went down hard and lost consciousness long enough for me to get David and flee. My attacker came to just as we were leaving." She tried not to think about the cold anger in his eyes when he came to, but the memory came unbidden and sent a shudder over her body.

"Can you describe him?" Blake asked.

Her stomach clenched. "He wore a ski mask, and I have no idea what his face looked like. He had dark brown eyes. And he's a big guy. Like Gage's height. Six-twoish. And I think he was limping. At least it seemed like it when he ran for the boat."

"Could be important...or not."

"How's that?" she asked.

"If it's a permanent limp, it could help ID him, but he could have simply hurt himself."

"Makes sense," she said, but she hoped it did indeed help find him.

"How much do you think he weighed?"

"I'm not good at judging that, but he was really built.

Like Gage. All muscles." She glanced at Gage who was eyeing her with the same unabashed interest he'd displayed often in their past, and heat crawled up her neck and over her face. Trouble was, she liked seeing the interest in his eyes back then and now, but he'd bailed on her and she'd never go down that path with him again.

"Did he speak?" Blake asked.

"He asked me if I thought he wouldn't find out and said he wouldn't let me destroy him. I have no idea what he meant, but maybe he was speaking of the reconstruction. Like if I finished the project, we'd recognize the woman, and he'd be caught."

"If that's the case, then he likely took the skull with him. I'll follow up with my deputy." Blake tapped his pen on his notebook. "Can you think of anyone who might have a reason to want to kill you?"

"Me?" Her mind raced over the past, grasping for anything. A nugget. Smaller even. Anything that could help locate her attacker. "I can't think of anyone."

"What about someone from another investigation where you did a reconstruction or drawing?" Gage asked.

Could someone really want to kill her? "I don't know. I mean, this is all so surreal and no one comes to mind. But I can hardly think. My mind is muddled. The pain. The shock of everything. I just...I don't know."

"What if your drawing of a suspect resulted in an arrest, and the suspect is seeking revenge?" Gage asked.

She considered his question for a moment. "I suppose that's possible, but again, nothing comes to mind."

Gage's narrow-eyed focus remained on her. "With what your attacker said, that theory would make sense."

She couldn't begin to acknowledge that someone wanted to kill her for any reason, much less a reason that wasn't connected to the skull. "He'd want to stop me from finishing the reconstruction, that's for sure."

"Both theories are valid," Blake said. "We could be looking at someone from your past or someone related to my investigation."

His phone chimed, taking his attention. He peered at the screen, then looked up. "My deputy found a boat with blue oars. Looks like it was secured in a cove down the shore a bit."

"This guy survived, then." Gage's eyes darkened.

"Oh, no! Before he took off, he said this wasn't over. He's going to come back, isn't he? Find me? Kill me?"

Gage's fingers curled into tight fists. "Not on my watch, he won't."

She looked at him and recalled the fierce protector she'd known. She'd always felt safe with him. Always. And her heart thrilled to hear he still wanted to keep her safe. But could she trust that? Trust him?

"I should never have convinced you to work on the skull," Blake grumbled.

"Hey." Hannah changed her focus to Blake. "Don't think that way. I chose to do the reconstruction, and I still plan to finish it."

"If your attacker didn't take the skull," Gage added.

"Right, but if it's still at the cottage, I'm glad to finish it. I'd take it to Portland, though, where this guy isn't likely to find me."

"He knows who you are, Hannah," Blake said. "It won't be hard for him to find out where you live."

"What? Right. Right. I suppose he does. I didn't think of that."

Gage crossed his arms and widened his stance as if setting a line. "Once you're released, you'll stay at the compound with me until your attacker is behind bars."

She opened her mouth to argue, but he held up a hand, stopping her. "Don't worry. We won't be alone. My daughter, Mia, and her nanny live in the main house and the rest of my team in cabins."

She shot him a questioning look. "Team and compound, seriously? Exactly what have you done since leaving the SEALs?"

"Right, you wouldn't know. I started my own business. An injury ended my SEAL career, and I couldn't find work I'd enjoy. That's when I discovered other guys with injuries that took them out of the military or law enforcement. Being married to a SEAL, you know how we all reacted to such a thing."

Boy, did she. "It would be worse than death."

Gage rubbed his right forearm and stared at the wall. Could this be where he sustained that injury he mentioned?

He shook his head and blew out a breath. "Anyway, I couldn't sit around and feel sorry for myself forever. So I gathered a team of these guys together and started Blackwell Tactical. I have five other professionals on the team and fifty acres where we train law enforcement officers. We also provide protection services for people in distress."

"That's the perfect solution while we look into the attack." Blake flipped his notebook closed as if he was closing the discussion, too. "Gage's compound is highly secure. And you'd be hard-pressed to find anyone better to fend off this attacker and keep you alive."

She supposed Blake was right. Gage *was* well qualified, but what Blake didn't have any insight on was how a simple look from Gage stirred up feelings she'd thought were long dead. The way her heart fluttered around him. The way she had to remain in protective mode while in his company. If she wasn't, she'd find herself falling for a man who'd left her in a lurch once, and she had no reason to believe he wouldn't do so again.

$\sim$

In a hallway restroom, Gage tugged the hospital scrub top over his head. He was glad to be dry, but the cotton shirt felt like it would rip at the seams if he so much as flexed his shoulders, and he wished his associate would get here soon with the things he needed to spend the night.

Spend the night. Crazy. Pure craziness. There he'd been —minding his own business—out for a nightly jog along the cove like he did every evening to clear his head. And then, Hannah and her son suddenly barreled into his world, making it all topsy-turvy. He tried to make sense of seeing her again and the emotions spinning through his body.

Even if they didn't have a past, what man wouldn't react to her? She was a beautiful woman. Fiery red hair that even after a dunking in the ocean looked soft, swirling around her face. Sparkling blue eyes. A round face that lit up when she smiled—which, granted she wasn't doing tonight—but he still hadn't been able to quit staring at her.

"Enough," he muttered and tossed his wet clothes into a plastic bag.

He left the restroom to pad down the quiet hallway. He felt vulnerable and foolish without his usual clothes, but at least he was warm and dry. He rounded the corner to Hannah's corridor. A large man, maybe six two, two-twenty pounds with a solid frame and wearing jeans and a hoodie pulled over his head stood outside her door. His hand rested on the handle.

Was he leaving or entering the room? And who was he?

Hannah said she didn't know anyone in town, and this guy matched the build of the man she'd described as her attacker. Plus he certainly looked like he possessed the strength to put those bruises on her neck.

Gage hurried toward the room, his gut clenching with each step. The man glanced at Gage. He couldn't make out the man's face, but when he saw Gage heading his way, the guy spun and ran.

"Hey, you!" Gage took off after him. "Stop."

The man flew like a gazelle until suddenly he clutched his leg and a lame gait slowed him a bit. By the time Gage reached Hannah's room, the guy punched the bar on an exit door and fled into the stairwell. Gage considered pursuing, but he had to check on Hannah first. The guy could have already been in her room.

Panic reared up as he pushed the door open. He found her settled in bed, her arm around David, the pair cocooned in blankets. They both looked up from a book with a black cat on the front.

Hannah met his gaze and held it as she'd often done in the two years they'd been together. "What's wrong?"

"Everything okay in here?" He made sure his tone was casual.

"We're reading *Splat the Cat*," David announced.

"Anyone bother you?" Gage asked.

"No, why?" Hannah's eyes widened.

Gage didn't want to worry them. He smiled. "Just checking. I need to make a quick call, and I'll be right back."

He popped out into the hallway and dialed Blake to relay the incident. "We need a deputy over here now."

Muttered words came through the phone. "I'll dispatch someone and come back to take a look at security video."

Gage searched the hallway. "No cameras on this floor."

"Right, but we can look at exit videos."

"The guy was wearing a hoodie to hide his face. Could mean he's smart enough to avoid cameras."

"We'll just have to see."

No way Gage would sit around and wait to see if Hannah's attacker had returned or would come back. No way. He disconnected the call and typed a group text to his team.

Meet me at the hospital ASAP. We're protecting a woman and her son from a killer.

4

The hallway outside Hannah's hospital room was pin-drop quiet the next morning. Exactly as it should be. Then why was Gage so wigged out that he couldn't stand still? Maybe it was because hospitals shouldn't be quiet. But he was the reason behind the silence, and he surely should be able to shake off this unease. He'd effectively closed off access to Hannah's room for the last five minutes by stationing former Army Ranger Cooper Ashcroft at the end of the corridor with instructions to rebuff anyone without a hospital security badge.

Gage was taking no chances with Hannah's life. He'd called in every team member. Eryn, the only female in the group and a former FBI cybersecurity professional, stood next to Hannah's door. Riley Glen who'd most recently joined Blackwell Tactical after a bullet ended his sniper career with the Portland Police Bureau along with former Green Beret Jackson Lockhart and former recon Marine Alex Hamilton all took formidable stances nearby as they waited for Hannah to prepare to depart for the compound.

Eryn glanced at her watch. "Shouldn't we be going?"

Gage thought the same thing, but he couldn't rush the

nurse in her after-care instructions. "We're good until someone complains about Coop blocking the hallway."

She nodded and widened her stance as if she felt the same anxiety as Gage. She wouldn't be defending anyone today but would serve as a stand-in for Hannah in a decoy vehicle while the rest of the team slipped Hannah and David out the service entrance in a plain white van. They'd rigged up a dummy that looked like a boy covered in a blanket, and Gage would carry the dummy to mimic holding David.

Gage resumed his pacing and ran the transport plan through his mind again for the hundredth time since he and the team created it last night. It hit him then. The reason for his anxiety. He wanted to be in the van with Hannah and David, not in the decoy vehicle. Too bad. He had no choice. If the guy outside her door last night was indeed her attacker, he would expect Gage to accompany her. If he had the hospital staked out, he would also expect to see Gage escorting her home. That meant Gage had to drive the decoy vehicle if they had any hope of confusing her attacker.

"You're gonna wear a hole in the floor." Jackson raised thick brows, the deep black matching his buzz cut.

Gage scowled at the guy about his same height.

"Hey, man." Jackson held up a hand. "It's the truth."

After a night sitting in a stiff recliner in Hannah's room and jumping every time someone entered to check on her, Gage was in a foul mood. The last thing he needed was for Jackson to remark on his pacing, even if Gage had hired the guy because he didn't pull any punches and spoke his mind.

Gage took a breath. Blew it out to keep his temper in check.

Jackson shook his head. "Your attitude seems like

overkill for simply moving a woman and boy five miles down the road."

Gage spun on him. "That's the kind of thinking that will screw up this op. Five miles or five feet—I need you focused and ready for the unexpected."

Jackson poked out his chest and settled large hands on his waist. "You calling my ability to do my job into question?"

Gage took a similar stance but widened his feet, too. "Do I need to?"

"Hey, hey." Shoving a hand in surfer-blond hair, Riley Glen stepped forward. "Why don't we take this down a notch? We all know how to do the job, and we'll be in top form at go time. You know that, Gage."

Gage *did* know that, but he couldn't shake this ominous mood. As Jackson said, this was a simple transport, and Gage needed to control his nerves or he could be the one to blow the op.

Riley faced Jackson, his expression placating. "And you know Gage respects your skills. If he didn't, you'd be long gone from the team."

"I suppose," Jackson grumbled and stood down.

Riley clapped Alex on the back. "We could use one of your stupid jokes right about now."

"Hey, I'm no standup. You get a joke when you get 'em." A smile curled up his mouth, but Gage didn't feel like smiling.

The door suddenly opened, and Hannah stepped out. Even though the doctor said the brain bleed was minor and cleared her to leave, Gage ran his gaze over her to make sure all was well. He had to admit except for bruises and scratches she did look good. He'd sent her wet clothes home for his housekeeper to launder last night, and it was the first time since they'd broken up that he'd seen Hannah dressed in dry street clothes. His gaze lingered on curves that had filled out since he'd last seen her, and his thoughts traveled places they had no business going.

"Ah-ha," Jackson said. "Now I get the angst."

Gage jerked his gaze free and introduced the team. Hannah shook hands with each person and looked them in the eye, not wavering when many people would feel intimidated by the sheer size and intensity of the men. David hung behind her leg and kept poking his face out to look up at them.

"You okay, little man?" Gage squatted down to smile at the boy.

"My daddy worked with big guys like you. And he had to 'fend our country. Are you 'fending us?"

"Defend," Hannah corrected, but she didn't answer his question. "I'd love to get out of here before they decide to keep me."

She tried to smile, but she'd only quirked up one corner when it flat-lined. He hated that. She was an amazing woman, and she didn't deserve to continue to suffer. Hadn't deserved the attack in the first place. But then, who did deserve something like that? Maybe getting settled and feeling safe at the compound would bring back her smile.

"Any questions on the plan?" he asked, though he'd reviewed their strategy multiple times with her.

She twisted her hands together. "Are you sure it'll work?"

Every op could go sideways, and he couldn't promise anything, so he nodded and left it at that. "Let's get moving."

"I wish you were going with us," David mumbled.

Gage forced out another smile for the boy. "I'll be at the compound before you know it, little man."

He squeezed David's shoulder, and then without thinking did the same thing with Hannah. She lurched back. Right. She didn't want him to touch her. Stung big time. Eyebrows rose on the team's faces, but they were too professional to comment.

"Let's move, people," he snapped to change the focus, and at their knowing looks, he wished he'd kept his big trap shut.

"Follow me, ma'am," Riley said.

"Hannah. It's Hannah. Okay?"

Riley nodded and smiled, accentuating good looks that Gage had seen women fawn over plenty of times. She didn't seem to notice but took David's hand and stepped off behind Riley. Gage took comfort in her reaction and hated that the thought had even entered his brain.

Alex strode next to them, and after an affirmative nod to Gage, Jackson took up the rear. When they reached the corner where Coop stood duty, he fell in on the other side of the pair.

Once in his vehicle with Eryn and the dummy, Gage would take evasive driving maneuvers to be sure no one followed them. His team in the other van carrying Hannah and David would follow similar tactics. They were all in contact over comms units and would meet back at the compound, but Gage didn't like seeing her disappear. Not even with four very capable men surrounding her.

"Let's go, boss man." Eryn pulled up her hood. Her dark hair was in direct contrast to Hannah's startling red color, and Eryn's face wasn't as round, but with the hood up and head down, she'd pass from a distance.

Gage picked up the dummy boy, and Eryn started off in front of him, a swagger in her step. Powerfully built from hours in the gym, she didn't have Hannah's soft curves or feminine walk.

Gage caught up to her. "Remember to walk like a girl."

"If only I *was* a girl and knew how to do that." She socked him in the arm.

"You know what I mean. You don't normally sway your hips as much as Hannah."

"You noticed her hips, did you?" Eryn smirked.

"C'mon. Let's move." Gage resisted responding and escorted Eryn to the elevator. She exaggerated her walk.

"Seriously," he said. "You do that outside, and I'm gonna clock you."

She laughed and despite his unease, he smiled.

At the front door, he patted his jacket to be sure his Glock was in place. Satisfied he was as protected as possible, he stepped onto the sidewalk, praying this killer was nowhere in sight.

The compound was exactly like the sheriff had described it, and from the backseat of the SUV, Hannah surveyed every inch of the place through the spitting rain. Jackson leaned out the driver's window and pressed his thumb on an electronic reader near a sturdy metal gate she'd expect to find at a top-secret fortress.

"Isn't this security overkill?" she asked, her hand nervously fiddling with a strap on David's car seat where he'd fallen asleep.

Jackson cast a glance in the rearview mirror. "Gage likes his privacy. And if that's not enough reason, our work requires us to keep a well-stocked arsenal that we don't want anyone to get their hands on."

Gage had mentioned his business was training law enforcement officers, but she didn't really get what that meant until now. And the privacy thing? Why did Gage need this type of privacy? A red flag for sure, and one that told her to be watchful until she figured it out.

They wound down a long driveway into a clearing

surrounded by tall pines. A log house sat to one side under a towering maple tree casting shadows over the building. The grounds were manicured and utilitarian, but there wasn't a single flower in sight. Masculine, she supposed. Still, the grounds looked like a normal homestead, and Hannah saw no evidence of the training facility.

Jackson opened one of three garage doors and pulled in. He'd no more than removed the keys when he hopped out. Alex to her left and Coop in the front seat followed suit. They stepped to the open door and formed a protective barrier, their expressions focused and frightening in intensity.

"Want me to carry the boy?" Riley asked from his seat on the other side of her, a ready smile following his words.

"I'd appreciate that." Hannah returned his smile. "He didn't get much sleep last night, and I'd hate to wake him."

Riley seemed like such an agreeable guy and less intense than the others. Though he still had a solid build, he was the only blond among them. Maybe his lighter coloring made him seem less intimidating, or was it his personality? She didn't know, but she felt as if she could relax around him. The others, including Gage, not so much.

He picked up David, and she followed them into the house while the other men moved outside and closed the garage door. She could only imagine what they were doing, but she suspected they were standing strong, their hands on sidearms, waiting for danger to rear its ugly head.

She couldn't imagine doing their job, but it gave her better insight into what Nick's life must have been like. Sure, she'd met his teammates who were all imposing, but they were talking and laughing at social functions, not in the fierce intensity of a life-or-death situation like this one.

Hannah stepped into a large kitchen with white cabinets and granite countertops. A short, plump woman came bustling into the room followed by a bashful little girl. Mia, Hannah assumed. She had wispy blond hair held back with a bright purple headband to match a T-shirt paired with khaki shorts and sandals. She looked to be about a year or so older than David, and she carried the same underlying look of sadness that Hannah often found in David's eyes.

"The poor dear, all tuckered out." The woman rested a hand on David's back and peered at Hannah. "I'm Opal Bailey, Mia's nanny and basic housekeeper. You must be Hannah and this is David."

"Yes." Hannah immediately liked this woman with waves of motherliness rolling off her.

"The precious thing hiding behind me is Gage's daughter, Mia. Say hi, Mia."

"Hi." The word slipped out in her squeaky little voice.

Opal turned to Riley. "Let's get David up to bed, before I show Hannah to her room." She whirled around and rushed through a family room, Mia's tiny legs running to keep up. She stumbled near the stairs, appearing to be dizzy, before righting herself.

At the end of a long hallway, they stepped into a warm and welcoming bedroom. Riley gently laid David on the bed.

"Thank you," Hannah said and received another kind smile before Riley departed.

Hannah settled David in, and then followed Opal to the room next door, painted a lemony yellow, a color that surprised her for a single male's home.

"Gage's mom decorated the room." Opal gestured at the space as if reading Hannah's mind. "Would you like to rest or have a cup of coffee with my freshly baked strudel?"

Hannah didn't want to be sleeping when Gage arrived. "Coffee, please."

They returned to the traditionally decorated kitchen,

and Hannah took a seat at the large granite island next to Mia, who still hadn't said anything except *hi*. Hannah waited for Opal to try to discuss the attack, but she didn't say a word and hummed while she went about cutting a large piece of strudel and pouring rich black coffee in a pair of handcrafted mugs. Hannah opened her mouth to ask Mia a question, but the girl scooted to another stool looking like a frightened puppy, so Hannah opted to remain quiet. Opal served them each a piece of strudel, with milk for Mia and coffee for Hannah.

Hannah felt utterly safe in Gage's compound, and with the safety, her appetite returned. She devoured the strudel and polished off the coffee.

"You like it, then?" Opal grinned.

"Sorry for inhaling it like that, but my appetite has come back."

"Another piece?" she asked.

"Would it be rude to accept?"

"It would be rude not to." Opal chuckled.

Hannah glanced at Mia who was watching her, and when Hannah looked away, the child forked a small bite of her food and chewed.

Hannah slid her plate across the island to Opal for a refill just as the door opened and Gage walked in.

"Right in time for some strudel," Opal said.

"Just coffee for me."

"Daddy." Mia hopped down from her stool and, in an awkward gait, ran to her father.

"Hey, Bug." A wide smile crossed his face, and he scooped her into his arms and turned in a circle.

She curled her arms around his neck. On one rotation, Hannah saw a soft smile of contentment on her lips. She let go of his neck and rested her head on his chest. "I missed you."

"I missed you, too." A faraway look claimed Gage's eyes, and a burning desire to know what he was thinking caught Hannah unawares.

She suspected his thoughts resembled hers much of the time. Like pondering how much easier parenting would be with a partner. Coaxing his child into a happy state when she missed her mother. Telling her it was okay to be sad, and even more importantly, telling her being happy didn't mean she loved her mother less.

Gage took a seat on the stool next to Hannah and settled Mia on his lap. Hannah retrieved Mia's strudel and milk and set them in front of her. She shot Hannah a suspicious look and eased back into her father's hold.

"*Thank you* is the right thing to say, Bug," Gage said to his daughter.

A sullen thank you came from her mouth. Though not heartily meant, Hannah smiled at the timid girl.

"Where's David?" Gage asked.

"Asleep."

"Not surprising. He didn't sleep very well last night."

"Which means you didn't either."

Opal placed the strudel in front of Hannah, and she took a big bite, taking the time to savor the tart raspberry flavor this time.

"No worries. I'm used to it." Gage took a long drink of his coffee. "Blake called. He said his team is done processing the cottage, and we can pick your things up."

Her appetite vanished, and she set down her fork.

"Now, don't you dare make Hannah go out there to retrieve her belongings." Opal planted her hands on ample hips. "You can take me, and I'll pack it all up for her."

"That's not necessary," Hannah protested.

"Necessary, no. But I insist." Opal's face firmed with resolve.

"Thank you." Hannah said. "Someday maybe I can pay you all back for your kindness."

"Nonsense," Opal said. "We're glad to help, aren't we, Gage?"

He nodded. "Besides, the doctor said you should rest."

"I will, but it feels so good to be safe that I want to enjoy it for a little bit."

Mia's eyebrow quirked in a question mark, and Hannah instantly regretted her words. She didn't want David to worry, and now she'd made this child worry.

"How old are you?" Hannah asked to change the subject.

Mia looked confused for a moment then muttered, "Seven."

"David is five. Maybe you can play with him when he wakes up."

The shy little girl didn't respond but turned her attention to her strudel again. Hannah had to admit that Mia's reserved manner deflated a bit of her happy mood. Children usually responded well to her, and she wasn't used to striking out with them.

Gage set Mia on the stool next to him and faced Hannah. "I need to head out and meet with the team. Maybe you'd like to come along and see the compound."

"I should be here when David wakes up."

"Don't worry about him." Opal jutted out her curvy hip where her hand still rested. "I'll keep an ear out for him."

"Then, yes," Hannah said, thinking fresh air sounded good. Going with this very handsome man who she'd once loved sounded even better.

"Great." He got to his feet. "Blake mentioned a few other things I need to bring you up to speed on."

Right, this wasn't a simple trip together, a chance to get fresh air. It was the opportunity to discuss how in the blink of an eye her life had been torn apart.

5

A cold wind whooshed through grass and leaves and the sun slid behind ominous clouds, but Hannah didn't care. She was glad to be outside...to breathe deeply without fear. She climbed into the small utility vehicle next to Gage. The wind bit into her body like an icy winter day instead of the end of summer. She shivered and Gage shrugged out of his jacket.

"Take this." He handed it to her.

She thought to argue, but Gage had always been a gentleman, and she knew he'd insist so she held her tongue. He rested the worn leather on her shoulders, his touch that had felt so safe yesterday now raising warning bells in her heart. His gaze lingered on hers, a message in the depths of his eyes she couldn't decipher. She desperately wanted to linger there. Wanted to figure out what he was thinking, but that was such a bad idea.

"Where exactly is this business you mentioned?" she asked to distract them both.

He turned his attention to the vehicle and got it started. "It's about a mile down the drive. I didn't want Blackwell Tactical anywhere near the house where it might frighten

Mia. I don't suppose you really want a tour, but I didn't want to talk in front of her."

"Actually, I *am* interested in seeing your property." She figured if his business was a ramshackle mess, it would tell her just how skilled he and his team might be in protecting them. Not that she expected Gage to do anything halfway, but people change. Especially people who had been through great loss, something she was an expert at.

They set off down the blacktop drive that soon turned into a rough gravel road. She nearly lost her balance and grabbed onto the side bar as they wound through thickly wooded grounds until they reached another heavy metal fence secured with a thumbprint reader. She had to admit the extra security made her feel even safer, but she still wondered about Gage's need for it.

Once inside the fence, a large steel barn-like building came into view. Just beyond it, she noticed a city street with building fronts made of wood resembling a Hollywood movie set.

He pulled up to the barn and parked. "Jackson is doing a close-quarters combat training inside, and I need to check in to make sure everyone arrived. Mind if I do that now?"

"Of course not." She climbed from the vehicle, her sore muscles now stiff from the cold. But she tried not to show the pain so Gage wouldn't whisk her back to the house.

They stepped inside the heated building. A series of walls about seven feet high divided the large room. Six men stood in a single line by what appeared to be a barricaded doorway.

Gage came to a stop next to her, the musky scent of his aftershave reminding her of the many times he'd held her close. She moved a step away, earning a raise of his eyebrow.

"What are they doing?" she asked to change his focus.

"This is a simulation of what these officers might find

when approaching a house holding a dangerous suspect. I'll have to wait for Jackson to finish running this drill before I can talk to him. Is that okay?"

She nodded and watched as the first man rammed the door and the men piled into the room. Gunshots sounded over a loudspeaker, startling her.

"I should have warned you. We use sound effects to try to simulate situations that could actually happen during a raid."

"No, stop!" Jackson's raised voice came from the other side of the wall. "Everyone back outside."

The men trooped out and stood waiting. Jackson, dressed in tactical gear matching the other men, stepped up to the guy who'd led the team inside. "The first guy goes in deep. If you stop at the doorway, it forces your partner to go around you—wasting valuable time—and keeps you from receiving solid backup."

"Roger that," the man said.

"The second you enter that door, stack left, and the next man stack right." Jackson cast an appraising look around the group. "Everyone got it?"

They nodded.

"Let's go again," Jackson said. "This time practicing with dry fire."

"What's dry fire?" Hannah asked Gage.

"They aren't using live ammo."

Jackson stepped back through the opening and reattached the door. "Go whenever you're ready."

The men lined up, and the leader burst through the door again, this time disappearing to the left. The second man moved in, too, and headed to the right just as Jackson told them. Their movements were precise and quick. Like a clipped dance.

The third man grabbed a grenade from his belt and

tossed it into the space. Smoke soon billowed over the wall. Gunfire followed. And chaos exploded like the grenade as men shouted and shots continued to fire.

"Foolish move, Williams," Jackson's voice rose about the noise. "You're dead."

Dead. If they were actually entering a home, a compound, any building with a combatant on the other side, the man would be dead. This was what Nick's life had been like. Breaking down doors. Running into gunfire. Danger lurking in every corner. One false move and someone died.

She'd been so afraid of losing Nick when he was down-range that she'd never allowed herself to think of the details of his days. But he was gone now and she let her imagination run wild. He'd lived his life like these men. Faced situations as dangerous as this one. Not just occasionally, but all the time. And when he'd come home and been distant, she hadn't understood. Not really. She loved him, but she'd made his life harder than it needed to be. Always begging him to engage. To let go of his sullen mood. Buck up and be part of the family.

Why hadn't she given him more space? Understood?

Oh, Nick, I'm so sorry.

Nausea roiled in her stomach, and she felt as if she couldn't breathe.

"I..." she said to Gage, but at his concerned look she almost lost it. She couldn't stay there. She raced for the door. Pushed outside. A lump rose in her throat. She gulped in deep, agonizing breaths.

Gage followed her and stepped in front of her. She couldn't look at him.

"What's wrong?" he asked.

She couldn't answer. With a gentle finger, he took her chin and lifted her head.

"I can help," he said softly. "Tell me."

"Nick…I…never…" Tears pricked her eyes. She drew in a breath and let it out. "I never understood his life. His need to decompress at home. I made it difficult for him. Complaining about how distant he always was. Now he's gone, and I can't tell him how sorry I am."

She clutched her arms around her stomach, trying to fight the sobs that wrenched from her body.

"Aw, honey." Gage gently pried her arms open and drew her into his.

She went willingly and cried into the solid wall of his chest until she could cry no more. Then she became aware of him. Of his heartbeat. His nearness. His warmth.

He retrieved a handkerchief from his pocket and handed it to her. Surprised, she blinked at him.

"I carry one for Mia. We always need to clean up something or other and carrying a purse with wipes is not an option for me." He grinned then, and as she imagined him with a purse, her mood lifted enough to return his smile.

"If it's any consolation, you aren't the only spouse who had a hard time dealing with the struggles members of the military have when coming home," he continued. "Combine that with the frequent absences of spec ops guys like Nick, and it's even harder."

He frowned, maybe thinking about his time as a Special Operations Operator. "I wish I could say I was the model husband and Cass didn't have to deal with this. I wasn't. We had some rough patches, but we toughed it out."

Her last day with Nick came flashing back. They'd fought and instead of working things out with her, he'd taken off. And had never returned. A sobering reminder of Gage bailing on her and the reason she couldn't depend on him. She pushed free of his hold.

"Nick likely understood," he added. "We all do."

"I'm not so sure about that. Before he died, our marriage was on the rocks. I like to think if he'd lived we would have worked things out, but I'll never know." Tears threatened again, and she bit the inside of her cheek to keep them at bay.

"I know your tenacity and unwillingness to give up on things that are important to you, and I'm sure you would have kept your marriage together."

"I gave up on you."

There was no mistaking the hurt in his eyes. "You had no choice. I got myself reassigned to the other side of the country." His eyes narrowed. "I'm sorry for the way I handled things back then. I was a real jerk. I could blame it on being young, but it was more than that."

She hadn't forgiven him for bailing on her and didn't know what to say. Plus with her emotions so raw, this was the last thing she wanted to discuss. "We should get going."

Gage eyed her for a long moment, then without a word escorted her to the vehicle. He didn't have to say anything. He carried his disappointment in his posture. Or maybe it was more than that. Maybe he really did regret leaving her back then, but what difference did that make now? None.

She settled on the worn seat and tugged his jacket tighter to keep out the wind.

He slipped behind the wheel. "I'm sorry I didn't come to Nick's funeral. I thought it would be awkward for you."

"That was considerate of you," she said making sure he knew she was sincere.

"If you don't mind me asking, how did he die?"

"He went hiking and rock climbing on his own. Fell off a cliff. I begged him to take someone with him, but he believed he was invincible. Maybe if he'd brought a buddy along that day, he'd still be alive."

"You can't think that way. I know. I've done it for the past

53

three years. Thinking if I'd been stateside I might have prevented the accident that took Cass and injured Mia. Does me no good. Just the opposite."

"I get it. Trust me. Get it big time. It's been two years since Nick passed away, and I'm still trying to figure out life without him." She held up a hand as he opened his mouth to speak. "I'm not feeling sorry for myself, and I know everyone has something to deal with. I'm not looking for pity, just saying I'm still finding my way."

"I wasn't going to say anything about pity. I was going to say that Cass died three years ago, and I still struggle with things." His lips tipped up in the sweet, soft smile, so contrary to this guy's tough and rugged exterior. "Like braids and ponytails. I don't know what I'd do without Opal."

Despite her angst, at the mention of the housekeeper, Hannah's mood lifted. "She seems wonderful."

"She's the best." He looked like he wanted to add something but changed his mind and got them moving down the short street.

"We tried to make this set as real as possible for our urban tactical classes," he said above the engine, but didn't slow down.

She took in the tree-lined street holding a bank, post office, grocery, and other retail stores. Even a Starbucks. "You did a great job."

They soon reached a bigger field with a small hangar and helipad. A chopper sat on the pad.

Gage stopped close by. "Our air assault classes are headed up by Coop. In the distance you can see our range where we teach shooting classes."

"This is impressive. Very impressive." She was about to ask for additional details, but an alarm chirped from his phone, drawing his attention.

"That's a reminder of a class I need to teach." He silenced it. "We should talk about my call with Blake."

She braced herself against news she didn't want to hear. "What did he say?"

"First, the skull is gone."

"Gone," she muttered and processed the news. "So my attacker *does* have something to do with that investigation."

"Not necessarily. He could have taken the skull to misdirect us."

"Really? Do you think he could be thinking that clearly when he was in such a rage?"

"I've run into a lot of cold-blooded killers over the years, and I've found that they often think clearly. Not rationally, but clearly."

The term cold-blooded killer flashed in her brain like a neon sign, and she could hardly process the words. "I know this guy attacked me, and if I hadn't gotten away...well...I haven't let myself go there, so I haven't really thought of him as a killer until now."

"I'm sorry to bring it up, but we have to face facts if we want to catch him, right?"

She nodded.

"Blake also discovered that the boat was reported stolen from a nearby town. His team lifted prints, but since you say he wore gloves, they won't likely pan out. DNA's another story. They were able to lift a blood sample from the hammer at the cottage, but it could take weeks to get the DNA results, plus the FBI database may not return a match."

"So what happens next"

"He'll keep after the forensics leads, but he wants you to make a list of investigations where you did reconstructions or sketches that led to convictions so he can look into them."

"You mean because the defendant would be angry at

me?" she asked as she pondered the implications. "Sounds like Blake really does think this is about me and not the reconstruction."

"He still thinks it's possible, and at this point he has to follow every angle." Gage cast an assessing look her way. "Think back to defendants who glared across the table at you. Did any of them threaten to get even with you or seem extremely angry? Or maybe one of them had a limp?"

She tapped her finger on her chin as she thought, but finally gave up. "No one comes to mind right now."

"Spend some time thinking about it. I'm sure you'll come up with someone." Gage squeezed her hand then got the vehicle moving forward again.

Concentrating so hard had left her head throbbing, and she rubbed her forehead to ease the pain.

How had she found herself in this situation? Someone wanted to hurt her. Kill her. Not because of the reconstruction, but perhaps because of something she'd done earlier. Her job for crying out loud.

Unbelievable. Crazy unbelievable.

If she didn't come up with the right name so they could locate and arrest her attacker, he'd keep coming after her, and maybe next time he would succeed.

6

Gage got up from the sofa and paced, his hand automatically drifting to the holstered Glock he'd strapped on the minute Mia and David had gone to bed. It wasn't likely that he'd need to use the weapon, but he wasn't taking any chances with Hannah's life.

Sure, he'd protect anyone needing his help, giving up his life if necessary, but such an overwhelming protective need had consumed him like this only once before. The day he'd heard about the drunk driver plowing down Cass and Mia.

He stopped near the dining room to peek in on Hannah. Sitting at the table, she was tapping a pen on her chin, the notepad in front of her holding several names. She met his gaze.

"Looks like you came up with a few people who might want to harm you," he said.

"I don't know." She twisted a long strand of hair between her fingers. "I mean, my attacker said he wouldn't let me destroy him, but I'm not trying to destroy anyone, and listing names seems like a waste of time." She let her hair fall as a pensive sigh slipped from her mouth.

He pointed at her list. "Who's your top suspect?"

She circled the first name. "Fitz Ellwood. He threatened me, but he had no reason to follow through on it."

Gage leaned against the doorjamb. "Tell me about him."

"He was accused of abducting two teenage girls and killing one. I was called in to meet with the girl who escaped to create his sketch. Once the police gave the sketch to the media, it was less than a day before they arrested Elwood. He glared at me in court and said if he was convicted, he'd get even." She shuddered.

"And was he convicted?"

She shook her head. "Sadly, no. So he has no reason to come after me."

"How long ago was this?"

"A couple of weeks ago."

"I wouldn't be this quick to write him off. If he really did murder this girl, I doubt he'd think twice about killing you for testifying against him."

"Still, I don't know." She ran her fingers over the names then suddenly looked up. "If you have a computer I can use, I could look up other trials to refresh my memory and maybe expand the list."

"Wouldn't you remember a man angry enough to kill you?"

"You would think so, right? But maybe his anger wasn't overt and details of an investigation might remind me of something."

"Makes sense." He pushed off the doorframe. "I keep top-level information on my office computer, and I don't use it to connect to the Internet, just my secured local network. But I do have an iPad you can use."

She tilted her head. "I've never used an iPad, so you'll have to help me."

"Glad to. It's in the family room." He waited for her to

come around the table and follow him into the family room where the iPad lay on the sofa table.

He sat, and she settled next to him. Her leg rested against his, the warmth firing all of his senses. How on earth would he manage to stay close enough to help her with the tablet and not want to act on his attraction?

You'll just have to deal with it.

He forced his focus to the iPad and gave her a speedy rundown on how to operate the device. Little puffs of her breath on his neck distracted him, and he all but shoved the device at her and shifted down the sofa. Oblivious to his meltdown, she started tapping away at the screen. He should look away, but he watched her work.

Memories of caressing her soft skin, of kissing those full lips, flooded his brain. He'd once been in love with her. Totally in love. But what did he feel now? It didn't matter, right? He couldn't even comprehend a relationship, much less entertain getting married again. Look how he'd reacted to losing Cass. He'd become a madman with a death wish. It had taken his father to snap him out of it.

He'd left Mia with his mother and gone on a bender. Dragged his sorry butt home and collapsed on the sofa. In the morning, his dad woke him up and forcefully sat him down. His father's words still echoed in his head. *Take care of your responsibilities, Son, or I'll take care of them for you. If that happens, precious little Mia will be out of your life for good.*

Gage didn't know if his dad would truly seek custody of Mia and cut him out of the picture, but the threat changed everything. He'd gotten it together and tried to be the best father possible.

But another relationship with a woman? No. That wasn't going to happen.

He'd stick to his work, which—for the most part—was neat and tidy. Step by step. Follow procedure and plans, and things usually worked out fine. Not so with relationships. There was nothing neat and tidy about loving another person. Nothing orderly. Just a messy jumbling of emotions that often ended in pain.

He shifted his focus to the iPad. A picture of a mid-thirties, handsome, and fit male filled the screen. He appeared to be an everyday kind of guy until you looked into his eyes. They were angry and mean, reminding Gage of killers he'd come across on deployments.

"Is that Ellwood or someone else?" he asked.

"Ellwood," Hannah all but whispered the name and clicked on another picture where Ellwood's bicep revealed a tattoo.

Gage recognized the sword and lightning bolts on a green background. "Tattoo says he was an army spec ops guy. Not someone I'll let anywhere near you."

"Thank you, Gage. For being here for me." She shifted to look at him, and when their gazes connected, his heart took a tumble.

He lifted his hand, ready to stroke her cheek. She didn't move. Not even to take her next breath. She felt the connection, too. It was still there. Strong. Nearly vibrating through the air.

A shrill alarm suddenly sounded from the iPad's speakers.

Hannah jerked back, her eyes wide. "Did I break it?"

"No." The special alarm came from the compound's security program. He took the iPad and silenced it, then clicked on the facility map and a red blip blinked at the south entrance.

"What's that?" she asked.

"Someone breached the south gate." He tapped the screen to bring up the live video feed from security cameras boasting night-vision capabilities. A tall, broad-shouldered male moved stealthily down the drive.

"Someone broke in?" Hannah's voice skated high.

"Looks like it." Gage made sure to keep his tone cool but grabbed his phone and dialed Alex who was the team expert in tactical tracking. "We have a breach at the south gate. I need to stay at the house with Hannah and—"

"You want me to track this loser," Alex finished for him.

"Affirmative. Take Jackson. His close-quarters skills might come in handy. And get Coop up to the house now to stand watch upstairs for the kids and Opal."

"Roger that."

"I'll be watching on camera. If you move out of range, I'll be on the comms, too. Let me know the minute you have the intruder in custody."

"Understood."

Gage disconnected and peered at Hannah whose eyes were wide with fear. He didn't want to add to her terror, but he had to make sure she remained safe.

He stood and held out his hand. "We're moving to an interior room without windows. My office is perfect." And it would let him grab his comms unit and watch the invasion play out over a larger screen, too.

"Is that really necessary?" Her face paled, and she placed a trembling hand in his.

"You have a guy who wants to kill you, and I've just experienced my first compound breach. Could be a coincidence, but I don't believe in them, and keeping you and the others alive is all I care about at the moment."

Thankful Coop had arrived to watch over Opal and the children, Hannah relaxed a notch and looked over Gage's shoulder at his large computer monitor where he'd brought up the security cameras on his network. She had a much better view of the man slipping into the compound than she'd had on his iPad, but it didn't matter. He never looked up to reveal his face, likely because he knew the cameras were there, so she couldn't tell if it was Ellwood.

"Does this guy fit the build of your attacker?" Gage asked.

"Yes." She continued to study the man moving with graceful stealth, and she could now see how he'd silently entered the cottage. "No limp. Maybe he's not our guy."

"Or maybe he's moving at a pace where it's not noticeable."

"One thing's for sure. He looks like he's done this before."

"Agreed." Gage slammed a fist on the desk.

Hannah jumped back. "What was that for?"

"This creep is making his way across my land, and there's nothing I can do about it. I feel as helpless as a little kid sitting here."

"I'm sorry, Gage," she said sincerely. "You could go after him if you didn't need to stay with me."

"Fat lot of good I'd do even if I was there."

Surprised at his answer, she came around the desk to see his face. "What does that mean?"

He sat staring ahead, not answering.

"Gage," she said softly.

His focus jerked back to her as if he'd forgotten she was there.

"You said you'd be no good to your team," she said again.

"Right." He pulled up his shirtsleeve and held out his arm. Angry, red scars crisscrossed his forearm.

How he must have suffered. Maybe still suffered.

Sadness for his pain seeped into her soul but she made sure not to show any reaction. "Your injury while a SEAL?"

"Actually, it didn't happen as part of my job, but I *was* downrange that night." His voice broke, and he took a few breaths, then shook his head as if clearing out the memory. "That was the night I got the news that Cass and Mia were plowed down by a drunk driver when he jumped the curb."

"Oh, Gage. I'm so sorry." He'd nearly lost both Mia and his wife. She couldn't even imagine the pain. "I know how it feels to lose a spouse, but having Mia hurt, too. That must have been rough."

He nodded, but his gaze cut away from her. "They both sustained serious head injuries and by the time I got home, Cass was in a coma. She stayed that way for months before she died. Mia still has long-term motor skill and speech impediments, and she's been withdrawn and reserved since the loss of her mother."

Hannah's heart broke for precious little Mia losing her mother and sustaining life-changing injuries, too. It explained why she seemed a bit off in her movements. Even her silence. Hannah offered a quick prayer for the child and hoped that God might hear and answer at least this one plea. "So that's when you left the SEALs?"

"You'd think I would, right? Come home and be the dad my daughter needed. But I didn't, and I'm not proud of it." His voice hitched with emotion.

"What happened?" she asked and held her breath in wait for his answer.

"I returned to duty right after Cass's funeral. An escape really. I left everything behind for my parents to deal with. Left my baby girl, too." His voice faltered again, and he paused. "But God saw fit to bring me home."

"God," she said, wondering how God was helping Gage when He clearly wasn't smiling on her. She had no idea if

He even loved her. "I wish I could say He was there for me when Nick died, but I just didn't feel Him nearby. But you. How did He help you?"

"By allowing the injury to my arm."

"Seriously?" She gaped at him. "How can you possibly think that was helpful?"

"Trust me, it's only in hindsight and after lots of soul-searching that I realized He could see things I couldn't. It still makes me angry that I can't do everything I need to do, but the injury brought me home to Mia and that's what's most important, right?" Gage locked gazes with her. "You look skeptical."

"I haven't felt God's presence in a while." A deep ache plagued her, but she shrugged it off as she'd done for some time. "But tell me about the accident and how it brought you home."

"After Cass died, I had a death wish. Didn't know it back then. I can see it now. I'd been deployed for so much of Mia's life that she didn't really know me. Add the brain injury, and I believed she'd be better off without me—better with my parents."

"But you came home."

"Yeah, after I injured my arm."

"But you said you didn't get hurt as a SEAL."

"Technically I was on duty—you're always on duty—but it happened when we had a couple of hours of downtime. I borrowed a motorcycle and went for a ride. Came back in an ambulance."

Hannah knew this personality. Knew it well. A daredevil, exactly like Nick.

"The docs did surgery and patched me up the best they could, but I messed it up pretty bad. The damage to my arm meant I wouldn't be doing anything but sitting at a desk for the navy. So I took the hardship discharge and stayed home."

"Mia needed you."

He scrubbed a hand across his jaw and released a long, pulsing breath. "She did, and I'd like to say I finally manned up, but I didn't. My injury kept me from getting a job in a field where I was qualified. I drowned my sorrows in a bottle first."

She nodded. "I can understand that."

"Understand it, but I'll bet you didn't run away from your responsibilities or fall apart when your husband died."

"No, but I can see how easily it could happen. So no judgment from me, okay?"

He nodded, his expression pensive.

"That's when you started this place." She gently touched his arm.

He looked at her hand as if determining how he felt about it, then continued, "Yes, thanks to my parents. After I told them about other guys I met in the same situation, my dad suggested I think of a business where I could employ them and he'd give me the land to house the business. A great offer, but making that decision wasn't easy either."

"Why's that?"

"The last place I wanted to live was here in Cold Harbor, settled down with a child. That's my parent's life, you know? If that was my dream, I wouldn't have to start a business. I could have run their grocery store. But I didn't want to live in this hick town. I wanted adventure. Travels. Which is why I enlisted in the navy to begin with."

"I think it's a lovely little town, and I shopped in the grocery store when I got here. It's a quaint, well-stocked place."

"I know that now, but back then, I was still in my see-the-world phase and couldn't recognize the goodness in my own backyard. You know, the same mode I was in when we split up. I couldn't get married then and settle down. I would have felt suffocated. I only agreed to marry Cass because she got pregnant."

Hannah's heart constricted. "So what you're saying is if I'd ignored my beliefs, slept with you and gotten pregnant, we would have gotten married."

He ran a hand through his hair. "First, I would never have asked. Second, I was immature enough back then that if you hadn't pressured me like Cass did, I still might have left." He swiveled in his chair and looked away.

She wanted to force him to face her. To work this out between them...but what was the point? She needed to stick to the matter at hand and hope she was able to leave the compound soon. "You were telling me how your parents offered to help you."

He turned and looked at her, and the anguish in his eyes almost had her taking his hand. Almost.

"Nothing much more to tell," he said. "I came up with the tactical training. Mom and Dad moved into town, and I used Cass's life insurance money to purchase start-up equipment and pay initial salaries."

"That was an honorable thing to do."

"Selfish, too."

"I'd say it was a win-win. You gave hope to men who needed hope, and you have gainful employment you love."

"True."

"How much can you do with your arm?"

He stared down at it as if it were an alien creature. "It works for most everyday things, but you could probably take me in an arm wrestling competition. Shoot, maybe even Mia could." He jerked his thumb at the monitor. "But without a doubt this guy could. Means I can't help in his capture in any way that doesn't involve using a weapon."

"How on earth did you manage to rescue me in a storm?"

"Adrenaline and dumb luck. It could easily have gone the other way." He clenched his jaw and turned his attention back to the screen.

End of discussion, which was fine with her. All this talk of their past wasn't going the way she'd thought it would the many times she pictured seeing him again. She had to admit his reasoning for not marrying back then was sound, and if they had gotten married, it would have likely ended badly. The way he handled the breakup was the real issue here.

"Report." He pressed his hand to his earpiece. "The intruder's out of camera range."

"I don't get it," he snapped. "How could he have evaded you?"

He listened, a frown turning down full lips. "Keep after him."

"What's happening?" she asked.

He met her gaze. "Somehow this guy caught sight of my men, and they spooked him into hiding. They're trying to locate him now."

"You said you don't believe in coincidences, but we were very careful not to let anyone see me arrive here. How can the guy who attacked me even know where I am?"

"Maybe he heard I rescued you, then saw on my website that we offer protection services, and he thinks I'm protecting you here."

"I guess that makes sense. If it *is* him, shouldn't you call Blake?"

He crossed his arms over his chest, looking formidable. "I can take care of my own business."

She thought his defensiveness had more to do with his lack of physical prowess because of his arm and less to do with being territorial. Either way, Blake needed to be informed. "If this man is here for me, then it's more than your business, right?"

He abruptly turned his head and pressed a finger to his ear. "Say that again?"

Okay. Fine. His team needed him. Maybe *she* should call the sheriff. But could she? Gage was doing his best to care for her and David, and she didn't want to go behind his back but...

"What do you mean you didn't capture him?" he snapped.

Hannah was glad she wasn't the one on the other end of the sophisticated device, as Alex's ear had to be ringing.

Gage jumped to his feet and paced like a caged tiger. He was fierce and strong. Even if his arm left him less than one hundred percent, he still had greater skills than most men. He was a warrior through and through, and the thought sent Hannah's heart beating faster.

"You're positive he's left the property?" He stopped to glare at the computer. "Then you get out there at dawn tracking him. I'll be breathing down your neck. And tell the team to count on doing recon trips outside the property at regular intervals starting *now* to make sure this guy isn't setting up camp on our doorstep."

7

Gage left his office for the family room, and despite the morning sun filtering through the window and brightening his childhood home, he remained on edge. Not unusual, he supposed. Typical behavior for when he was running an op. As much as he cared for Hannah, first and foremost, this *was* an op, and he had to keep reminding himself of that before he got distracted and someone got hurt.

At the family room door, his feet stilled at the picture in front of him. Hannah sat on the sofa, one of Mia's favorite books in her hands. David snuggled tight on one side, while Mia sat as stiff as a toy soldier about a foot away on Hannah's other side.

Mia's stiff little body, the downturn of her mouth that reminded him of Cass, broke his heart. Could there be anything worse in the world than seeing your child in pain and be helpless to fix it? If there was, he hadn't experienced it and hoped he never would.

"Your turn to flip the page, Mia." A smile on her face, Hannah held the book out to Mia.

Unmoving, his daughter peered up at Hannah.

Gage held his breath in wait for his daughter's response.

She didn't take well to strangers, and the fact that she was even sitting this closely to Hannah was a good sign. But interact? Not likely.

Mia lifted her hand.

That's it, Bug. Do it. Participate.

She dropped her hand to her leg and looked away.

"That's okay, sweetheart, I understand," Hannah said softly. "I was just as hesitant when I was a little girl. Let me know when you're ready. Okay?"

Mia blinked her responding yes, and Gage wanted to go scoop her into her arms and kiss her pudgy cheeks, but her therapist said coddling her all the time wouldn't help her learn to venture out of her own little world.

"I can turn the page for you," David offered. "You can do the next one."

Gage's heart swelled at David's kindness and his lack of belittling. Many children Mia's age teased her when she refused to interact in a group. The mean behavior made her problem worse. Maybe having Hannah and David staying here would be good for her.

He stepped into the room. All eyes peered at him. A tiny smile lit Mia's face, worry flooded Hannah's eyes, and David had big question marks in his. Hannah couldn't tell David about the attack, and he didn't understand why they'd left their wonderful vacation cottage to stay here. Gage needed to offer something fun for the boy to do so he didn't miss out on his entire vacation.

Gage focused on David. "Mia has a fort out back with ropes for climbing and swings, too. Maybe after your mom finishes the story, the two of you can go out to play."

David cast a hopeful look at his mother. "Can we?"

She questioned Gage with a look of pure anxiety.

He winked at her. "Rumor has it that Coop has missed swinging, and he wants to come out with you."

"Nu-uh," Mia said. "Coop's a man. He doesn't play."

"Sure he does. You just haven't seen him. You go back to your story, and I'll call him." Gage got out his phone and stepped into the hallway. "I need you at the house to keep an eye on the kids while they play outside."

"Sure thing."

"Neither one of them can know what's going on, so I told them you've missed swinging."

A groan filtered through the phone. "You know I'd give my life for you, but this? Man, you're pushing it."

"But you'll do it for Mia."

"Sure. I'll do it for the little squirt. But there better not be any pictures taken or so help me I'll—"

"See you in a few." Chuckling, Gage hung up.

Coop soon arrived and escorted Mia and David outside. Gage stood next to Hannah at the window to watch as the kids approached the large fort that Gage and the guys had constructed for Mia.

"Maybe I should have built a playhouse or something more feminine for Mia. I'm kind of lost on little girl things without Cass. Still, those stereotypes are gone these days, right?"

"Right, and I'm sure as long as you love Mia, and I can see that you do, she won't suffer from having a fort instead of a playhouse."

Mia and David both went toward the same swing, but David stepped back and let Mia take a turn first.

"You've got a great kid, there," he said. "I appreciate his kindness toward Mia. People don't often understand her limitations, and she gets hurt. Especially by other kids."

Hannah turned to look at him. "David's become more compassionate since Nick died. I hate that he lost his dad, but at least some good has come from it."

"Just what God promises," Gage said, and wished he could see the good more often.

She tipped her head up. "Since when have you become such an optimist about God and life's problems?"

He turned to look at her. "After I made peace with losing Cass, I found it helped. But before you think I'm a saint or something, I fail more than I succeed."

"Peace." She scoffed. "What's that? I'm still trying to figure out why we have to face such terrible tragedies in the first place. Why God would allow them."

"It's not ours to know. We just have to keep moving. Put one foot in front of the other and trust that God can see further ahead than we can. He has our best interests at heart, and it will all end up good for us."

"I don't know if I can do that..." She genuinely wished she could. "Not anymore. I'm not even sure He loves me."

Gage watched her carefully, unsure if he should continue. His heart ached for her. How could she not realize God loved her?

"You look like you want to say something," she said. "Go ahead. Say it."

"I'm beginning to sound like a preacher here, but maybe something my pastor told me can help you, too. He said that we learn to trust by experience. We need to recall all the times God has brought us through difficult situations. Remembering builds trust. Sometimes, down the road, we can see the reason. Often we can't."

"You mean like now? Like when someone wants to kill me? How do I trust He will keep me alive? Or David? He took my husband so...how can a loving God even do that?" Tears glistened in her eyes.

Gage's heart creased with her pain and he couldn't just ignore her tears. But he also couldn't take her into his arms. He'd compromise by taking her hand. "God didn't take Nick

—he knowingly made an unwise decision to go climbing alone. But I have to believe God saw fit for me to find you at the beach and put you in my care. I don't take that responsibility lightly. I have an amazing team, and we'll do our very best to make sure you and David aren't harmed."

She sniffled and gave a clipped nod as she extracted her hand. She shoved it into her pocket and looked down at her feet.

He'd dumped a lot of info on her and it was time to move on. "I called Blake, and I'm heading out to meet him at the gate that was breached last night. Opal went into town to get groceries, but she left the coffee maker on. Eryn's grabbing some now, and she'll stay with you."

"Thank you," she said, and he heard her sincerity. "I don't know what I'd do without all of you."

"You'll never have to figure it out. We're here for you until this is resolved." He lifted a hand to tuck a wayward strand of hair behind her ear, but he had no right to touch her like that. He'd lost that right when he'd walked out on her so he shoved his hand into his pocket. "I'll be back as soon as I can."

He left the house and headed down the path in the utility vehicle. He couldn't help but think of all of Hannah's wonderful characteristics. Warm, compassionate, loving. His feelings for her were growing by the minute, and he wished they didn't have to be together so often. But honestly, he didn't trust her care to anyone else for extended periods of time, so he would have to find a way to be in her company while keeping her at a distance. But man, when tears filled her eyes—when she was this sad, couldn't he just give her a hug?

No, he couldn't—and not want more. Meant he better find the guy targeting her so they could go their separate ways again.

He parked near the fence and followed small red flags placed in the ground to an area where Alex squatted next to Blake.

"Anything?" Gage asked.

Alex looked up. "Print pattern suggests tactical boots."

"You're thinking we're dealing with military."

"Or ex-military," Alex said. "Especially with the way the guy moved."

"I watched the video feed a few times today, and I have to concur," Blake said. "He's definitely been trained in evasion techniques."

"Ellwood was Army Special Forces."

Blake frowned. "You're not going to like hearing this. I asked Portland police to question him, but he's in the wind."

Concern raced along Gage's nerves. "Then he could be in town. Could be the one we're looking for. Not good. Not good at all."

Alex grimaced. "Sorry we lost him, man. I don't know how it happened."

Gage wanted to yell at him, but what good would do? Everyone made mistakes. "Even further evidence that the guy's not some hack but has strong evasion skills."

Blake nodded. "I need you to keep your team away from the boot prints until after I get someone out here to cast them."

"How will these casts help?" Gage asked.

"Sometimes narrowing down a shoe brand can lead to a suspect. At a minimum, it'll be useful in court when we catch this guy."

Gage planted his hands on his waist to keep from fisting them in frustration. "How are we standing on that?"

"The cottage is a rental. Means we have a large number of prints to process. So far, none of them returned a match in our database. Same with the boat. And if he wore gloves the entire time, none of them will."

"What about the boat registration?" Alex asked.

"As I mentioned, the sheriff told me the owner had already reported it stolen."

Gage eyed Blake. "And you're gonna trust his word?"

Blake cast him a baleful look. "I may not have traveled the world like you all, but I do know how to do my job, you know."

"I know, it's just..." Gage ran a hand through his hair. "I'm used to dealing with situations like this, but not in my own hometown."

"You still think of Cold Harbor as the ideal little world you left when you took off for the navy. Crime is everywhere these days. Even here, but we've kept it under control."

Gage may have traveled extensively, seen and done things that many people couldn't begin to imagine, but now that he'd accepted—even embraced—being home again, he wanted his small town to be safe. When this was all over, he would ask Blake if there was anything he and his team could do to help keep it that way.

"I should also mention," Blake continued, "that I have a lead in Jane Doe's investigation that could potentially direct us to Hannah's attacker."

"Tell me."

"When we found the body, we sent in hair samples for isotope research and bone samples for DNA testing. I received the isotope information this morning. It lets me pinpoint the victim's location for the two months leading up to her death. During that time, the information says she moved between warm and cool climates."

"A transient?"

"Maybe, or she could have a warrant out for her arrest, and she was avoiding prosecution."

"What about a migrant worker?" Alex asked.

"I'm not ruling that out," Blake said. "But the DNA tests helped determine her personal traits, too. She was most likely Caucasian of western European descent and not the typical race for our area migrant workers."

"DNA can tell you that?" Alex asked.

"It can even be used to digitally create a sketch of the subject's face, but due to cost, we decided to go with Hannah." Blake frowned.

Gage knew what the man was thinking. "After all that's happened to her, you're wishing you'd gone with the digital image, right?"

"Right." Blake's heated gaze met Gage's. "Promise me you won't let this jerk get to her."

"All I can promise is that I will do my very best."

The rest was up to God, and Gage had to find the strength to trust that what God wanted and what he wanted were the same thing.

~

Hannah remained at the window overlooking the backyard watching David and Mia run toward the large wooden fort. Hannah thought to go outside to warn David to be careful of the height, but she couldn't protect him every minute.

Hannah heard footsteps and turned to find Eryn carrying two coffee mugs. She lifted one toward Hannah. "Gage told me you liked your coffee black."

"Thank you." Hannah smiled and accepted the cup, but uneasy feelings about having David outside, even with Coop at his side, meant it was forced.

"You're worried about David," Eryn stated.

"Does anything get past the members of your team?"

"Actually, this has nothing do with the job. It's a mom

thing." Eryn gripped the cup hard, her fingers tuning white. "I lost my husband when my daughter was two. Now I go through life concerned I might lose her, too. Makes me worry about her more than I should." She frowned. "I hate to admit it, but I've become kind of a helicopter parent."

"You have a daughter, and you live *here*?" Hannah couldn't hide her surprise. "Sorry. That sounded judgmental. I'm not saying you're a bad mother and have your daughter living in a terrible place. I meant, how hard it must be to do this difficult job and have a child living here, too."

"Actually, it's fine. I pretty much work on computers, and —for the most part—Gage schedules me for a regular nine-to-five shifts. He's also great about working around any special needs I have."

"So you have daycare arranged?"

She nodded. "Bekah's four now, and she goes to preschool every day. My mom watches her for the rest of the time and when assignments take me out of town. And you can't beat the free living quarters that Gage provides for us."

This all sounded like the Gage Hannah once knew. In fact, until he'd bailed on her, she liked and respected most everything about him. Not something she would share with Eryn.

"Your mom sounds very helpful," Hannah said. "I never knew my father, and my mom passed away before David was born."

"It must be tough not to have a support system. But Gage says you're a strong woman and can handle most anything."

Oh, does he? "What else does he say?"

"Um, nothing else. At least not with words. But with the way he looks at you...well...the way you look at him, too, I suspect you two were once together." She met Hannah's gaze again. "Am I right, or am I prying too much?"

Hannah should have realized that this very intuitive

77

team wouldn't miss the dynamics between her and Gage. She'd tried to be careful to hide any emotions regarding him, but obviously, she hadn't managed it. "I don't mind telling people we were once a couple, but the reason for our split is private."

Eryn nodded. "Do you ever want to get married again? I don't specifically mean to Gage but married in general. I miss the closeness and being able to share everything with my husband." Tears glistened in her eyes. "But I can't even think about it, you know? I couldn't go through the pain of losing someone again."

"It's totally unlikely that I'd take the plunge again. But if I did, I sure wouldn't marry a man who puts himself in danger like Nick did as a SEAL." Hannah paused, surprised that her typical response didn't trigger the same vehemence it did before reconnecting with Gage.

"Then I guess Gage is out. Protection details put him in all kinds of danger." She shrugged. "Too, bad. I'd like to see you two get together. It's nice to have another woman on the property. Especially one I seem to have a lot in common with."

With all the testosterone flowing around this place, Hannah was enjoying talking to Eryn, too. But even if Hannah could easily fall for Gage again, Eryn's reminder of the danger Gage continued to put himself in gave Hannah one more reason to resist.

8

The scream was high and shrill. Mia! It was coming from Mia in the backyard. Felt like a big-bore bullet to Gage's gut, ripping him raw. He jumped from the utility vehicle and charged around the house.

David lay facedown on the grass in front of the fort, Coop kneeling next to him and assessing his injuries. Mia stood at the top landing of the fort, her face stark white. Gage wanted to go to her, but first he had to find out what happened to David. Gage raced across the lawn, and Hannah burst through the back door with Eryn.

Gage reached David first and squatted down. "What happened, Coop?"

Coop's eyes were dark with concern, and nothing ever spooked him. "David climbed onto the rail to reach for a squirrel. He fell before I could even warn him to get down."

David turned over and a long moan escaped his lips.

Hannah knelt next to him. "Son, are you okay?"

Her soft, pleading voice wrenched Gage's heart, and in that instant, he would do anything to take away her fear and pain.

David's chin wobbled as if he might cry, and his eyes misted. "My arm hurts."

"I think it's broken," Coop said. "I'll get the first aid kit."

"Let me see." Hannah took one look at the arm and clamped her mouth closed.

"Are you mad at me, Mommy?" David's tears seemed imminent now.

She smoothed back a lock of his hair. "You know what you did was wrong?"

"Yes."

"And you promise never to do it again?"

"Yes."

"Then I'm not mad." She pressed a kiss on his forehead. "But we'll need to go back to the ER to have you checked out."

"No. Mommy. Please. Do we have to go? I..."

"I'm afraid so, Son."

"I'll go with you." Mia's voice came from behind.

Gage spun to see her standing behind him, clutching her well-worn doll. The last place he wanted to take her was to the ER. She liked hospitals about as much as he did, but Gage would foster the interest she seemed to be developing in her new friend.

"I'll carry David," Gage offered.

Mia looked at him with a serious expression. "And I'll hold his hand."

He smiled at his daughter and couldn't get over the change in her normal timid behavior. "Then we have a plan, Bug."

Hannah kissed David's forehead again. "Here's Coop—he's going to wrap your arm up. Okay?"

"Ow! Ow!" David yelped as Coop carefully moved his arm to splint it.

Hannah's face pinched like she was the one in pain, but she soothed her son, and he quieted down. Gage gently picked the boy up and headed for the driveway. Mia held David's good hand and Hannah stood to Mia's side, her hand resting on Mia's shoulder. Gage was touched seeing Mia come out of her shell and warm up to David—and Hannah, too.

Coop hurried up next to him. "I'm sorry, Hannah. Gage. This wouldn't have happened if I'd gone into the fort with the kids."

"You're too big, silly," David said.

"Right." Coop smiled but focused on Gage. "Are we good, man?"

Just like Coop. Like *all* the members of the team. Putting other peoples' safety first and when someone got hurt, blaming themselves. Gage did the same thing, but Coop had no responsibility in this injury.

"Remember when you were a kid?" Gage asked. "How fast things happened and you or your friends got hurt?"

"Yep. Had my share of broken bones."

"Me, too," Gage said. "You're not to blame."

"It may have happened with all of us out here," Hannah added. "No need to feel bad, Coop."

He gave a firm nod of acknowledgement. "Mind if I ride along to make sure David's all right?"

"Glad to have you. In fact, I'd appreciate your help." Gage sent silent signals to Coop reminding him of the need to protect both David and Hannah on the drive.

Coop nodded and moved around the car.

Gage briefly considered sending out a decoy vehicle, but Hannah's attacker couldn't have seen David fall and couldn't possibly expect them to be leaving the compound. And the routine patrols on the road all morning found no sign of the intruder.

Still, Gage turned to Eryn who was standing by the front door. "Ride shotgun."

Gage wanted to say more, but he didn't need to scare the others, and Eryn was smart enough to figure out that Gage wanted her eyes and ears on the area for the drive.

"Mom says I can ride shotgun when I'm tall enough to sit in the front seat," David announced.

Good. He didn't think anything of Gage's comment.

"I'd be glad to have you by my side when you can sit in the front."

"Really?" David asked. "Can I do what your team does, too? They carry guns. I saw Coop's. He's hiding it, but I saw it when he lifted Mia to the top of the fort."

Gage opened his mouth to respond, but what should he say? First, David wouldn't be here for long, something Gage hadn't considered when he'd spoken. And a gun? Gage thought boys could be taught how to use a weapon responsibly, and he'd be glad to teach David when he was older, but he was sure Hannah would hate that.

"That's not something you need to think about." Hannah used her thumb to wipe a dirty smudge from David's cheek. "We're just visiting, remember? We'll be going home soon."

"Aw, I like it here. Mia's fun and I *love* the fort."

"Even if you fell out of it and broke your arm?" Gage carefully settled David in his car seat while everyone else took a seat.

"Yeah." David's voice held such excitement that Gage really wished the boy could stay. He patted David's head, then gave Mia a kiss on the cheek to reinforce her brave behavior.

As he backed out, David said, "You're a good dad."

The longing in David's tone froze Gage in place, and again, he didn't know what to say.

"Can you sit by me?" David asked.

82

"No, he can't, sweetie," Hannah said. "He has to drive."

His lower lip came out in a pout. "Wish he could sit next to me."

"Sorry, buddy. This is my car. I need to drive." David seemed to buy the apology, and Gage moved to the driver's seat.

He wouldn't have minded sitting by David, but even with a bum arm, he was still the best defensive driver on the team. He slipped behind the wheel and got them on the road. Gage and his team members didn't let their guard down and kept a watchful eye all the way to the ER. They sat in the waiting room for two hours before a nurse took David back for an exam. The minute David left, Mia snuggled up against Gage, and he held her close. If she was feeling only a smidgen of his unease at being in a hospital again, she was highly unsettled inside.

"Don't worry, Bug." He stroked her soft hair worn in curly ponytails courtesy of Opal. "David will be fine."

She nodded, but each time the door opened, she sat up to check for her friend then fell back against Gage. Man, he wanted to protect his little sweetheart. Not only from all danger in life, but also from her difficult emotions. His gut twisted. Those feelings extended to the woman and boy inside, too. If he hadn't bailed on Hannah, David would be his son. What a punch to the gut that was.

Mia squirmed, grabbing his attention. If he hadn't left Hannah, he wouldn't have his precious Mia. Not something he could ever imagine.

He scooped her onto his lap, and she rested her head against his chest, clutching her doll tightly. He kissed the top of her head. "Love you, Bug."

"Love you too, Daddy." She inched even closer, and peace settled in his heart like a warm blanket in the middle of an icy winter. But why now? Was it because David had gotten hurt and he was thankful for Mia's safety? One thing was for sure. The feeling had only occurred a few times since losing Cass.

Felt good after years of turmoil. He wanted more of it. Was this a sign from God? A sign that it was time to move on from mourning Cass?

The doors swung open, and David emerged with Hannah at his side. Her eyes were narrowed and tight, holding all the stress she'd been under. David's forearm held a splint covered in an elastic bandage. Either he hadn't fractured his arm, or the splint was temporary until the break could be set.

Mia hopped off Gage's lap and ran across the room to David. Gage tracked her with his gaze, his mouth falling open.

"She sure seems to like David," Coop said. "Never seen her this enthusiastic."

"She's changed all right," Eryn agreed.

And in only a few short hours. Apparently, all they'd needed to help her open up was a kind child who didn't gawk at or point out her differences. Not that Gage blamed other kids she'd played with for being unkind. Kids often focused on differences until they could make sense of them. Some went further and belittled, but even the innocent questions had hurt Mia.

Gage got up and joined them. "Are we good to go?"

"I broke my arm. Gonna get a cast," David announced, a gleam in his eye. "Orange one."

Gage wouldn't tell the little guy that once the cast got in the way or started itching, it would lose its luster.

Hannah sighed. "I need to get him in to see a pediatric orthopedist."

"I can help with that." Gage smiled to ease her worry, but she frowned. "Right now we should get back home. Opal must be back from the store by now, and she'll serve up big bowls of ice cream."

"Yay," David jumped up and down, but quickly stopped when a grimace of pain passed over his face. Mia did a dance in her awkward gait that Gage found completely adorable.

He scooped her up into his arms and turned to Coop to give a quick nod of his head. Coop understood and headed out the door to bring the car around. Another nod, this one for Eryn, and she went outside to evaluate the area for a safe departure.

Once Gage got the "all clear" from her, he hustled the others into the vehicle. Coop rode shotgun this time, with Eryn and Hannah in the third seat, the kids in the middle. He glanced in the mirror to make sure everyone had buckled in and traded a *be-alert* look with Eryn and Coop.

A kid's broken arm or not, Hannah's attacker was still out there waiting, and she was no safer now than she'd been before David's fall.

∽

Hannah's stomach hurt. Deep down. A cramping, nauseating feeling that wouldn't abate. Eryn had nailed things on the head. Hannah was being overprotective. Way overprotective. In fact, she now wished she hadn't allowed her son to play outside. What was next? Did she intend to put him in a bubble? Keep him with her twenty-four seven? He'd be an anxiety-ridden child in no time if she headed down the helicopter parent route, but she didn't know if she could handle anything else going wrong.

This wasn't about her, though. It was all about her precious son. About what was best for him. He needed her to stay strong. To not overreact. As Gage had said, kids get

85

hurt. And they did. All the time. That thought only made matters worse and raised so many questions. Like...was Gage right that God wanted the best for her? For David? How could a broken arm be good for any of them? Well, maybe it'd been good for Mia by the way she'd opened up.

Hannah glanced at the sweet little girl in the middle seat, still holding David's hand in the car. How incredible that she reached out to him, and that he continued to let her hold on. Maybe this *was* good for David, too, and even for Hannah. After all, it got her thinking about God in a different light. Perhaps Gage wasn't completely wrong.

Maybe. At least not in this area. But an earlier comment at the hospital about her and David staying in Cold Harbor? That was way off base.

David's head drooped and didn't come back up. Poor baby had fallen asleep from the excitement. Hannah leaned her head back and closed her eyes. Sleep beckoned, but her brain wouldn't shut down, and Gage infiltrated her thoughts. Being with him again reminded her of all the reasons she'd fallen in love with him in the first place. He was caring. Compassionate. Generous. Willing to go to the ends of the earth for the people he loved. To that, she now had to add doting father and a man who opened himself up to care for and help David. A boy who just a few days ago was a stranger.

She pried open her eyes and looked at him behind the wheel. Confident. Sure. Strong. Like Nick in those respects. But Nick wasn't a family man. He was a SEAL through and through, something she really hadn't noticed until after they'd had David. Gage on the other hand...

"Stop it," she said then clamped her hand over her mouth when she drew everyone's attention. "Sorry. I didn't mean for that to slip out."

Gage's eyes connected with hers in the mirror and

86

locked in place. Worried he'd read her thoughts, she jerked her gaze away and focused out the window.

She spotted a deer bounding out of the woods heading in collision course with their vehicle. "Look out! Deer!"

Gage swerved the vehicle, tossing Hannah toward the door. At the same time, the window above her shattered.

"Down!" Gage shouted. "Everyone down!"

Eryn shoved Hannah toward the floor, then threw herself over Hannah.

"What is it?" she cried out and tried to rise. "David! I have to get to him."

She heard David's fearful cry and Gage calming both of the kids.

"David's fine, but a bullet shattered your window," Eryn whispered, likely to keep from scaring the kids. "If Gage hadn't swerved...well...you...let's just say that bullet was meant for you."

9

Gage's whole body vibrated with rage as he stood by the kitchen counter while Opal scooped rocky road ice cream into bowls for the kids. He was an ice cream lover, especially any variety of chocolate, but the cream would curdle in his stomach right now. He was surprised David and Mia were still interested in eating it. Of course, no one discussed the bullet with them, and they only thought they'd been in a near accident because of a deer.

"If you don't mind, Opal." Gage forced out a smile and ruffled the kids' hair. "I'd like to leave these two hooligans with you while I talk to the team."

"What's a hooligan?" David dug into a big scoop of rich chocolate.

"Nothing you need to think about," Hannah said to her son. "I'll be joining Gage, so you be good for Opal, okay?"

He smiled up at his mother. "Hard not to be good when I have ice cream."

Gage smiled in earnest as he stared at the boy's bright eyes. Warm affection followed, settling deep in Gage's soul. David was such an amazing kid, but it was more than that for Gage. He was really coming to care for this boy. Wanted to see him succeed. Become the man Hannah no doubt wanted him to be. No wonder Mia blossomed around David. He was a special kid for sure. And Gage had to make sure he remained safe under his watch.

He gestured at the door for Hannah. She hugged David then started down the hallway. Midway to the office, she sagged against the wall, her chin quivering

"Hey," he said coming around to face her. "What is it?"

"A bullet. Someone fired at me." Her wild-eyed gaze darted around the space. "I couldn't let David see me this way, but I'm scared, Gage. So scared."

A lone tear slipped from her eye and ran down her cheek. Gage gently wiped it away and took her hands. "I won't let anything bad happen to you."

"You'll do your best. I know that. And your best is better than most people's, but still...if...the deer, if he hadn't been...the shooter could have...David. Poor, sweet David. He might be alone. An orphan. I..." Her words faltered and tears streamed down her cheeks.

"Aw, honey, don't." Gage released her hands and swept her into his arms.

She didn't fight him, but readily stepped closer and clutched his shirt as her back rose and fell in anguished sobs. He tightened his hold, wanting nothing more in life right now than to keep her safe. To keep David safe, too. For her. For Mia. For himself.

Man, had he fallen for Hannah again? He could totally see them as a family. The four of them. On picnics at the beach. Playing in the park. Grilling out for dinner with family games to follow.

She pushed back and planted her palms on his chest. "I'm sorry."

"Don't be," he said. "I'm here for you as long as you need me. You know that, right?"

Her eyes flashed up to his, fresh anguish overflowing in her gaze.

"I suppose you can't trust that, can you? Not with the way I bailed on you." He had no right to be holding her—to consider a future with her when he'd badly hurt her. "I'm sorry, Hannah. More sorry than I can ever convey and I hope that you can forgive me."

"I...I—"

"You needed my help, boss man?" Eryn rounded the corner and came to a halt. "Oh, sorry. I'm interrupting."

Hannah pushed away. "No. It's fine. What did you need Eryn's help with?"

Gage dragged his gaze away to focus on Eryn. "The shooter knew we would be on that road this afternoon. Either he saw us leave, or he's somehow tracking Hannah. Her phone is a logical tool for him to use as a tracking device, and I want you to look at it."

Eryn's ready smile lit up her face. "That's easy enough to do."

"I'll grab my purse, then, and meet you in the office." Hannah raced away as if her attacker was chasing her.

"Um, sorry again for interrupting," Eryn said.

"It was nothing," Gage replied, but suddenly it *was* something. Something big. Something he had no control over, and for that very reason, he couldn't keep thinking about Hannah in this manner. He would have to consider her a client. Simply a woman needing his protection.

He pointed at the office door for Eryn. "The team's waiting for us."

He followed her into the room where team members sat in leather easy chairs, and Coop perched on the corner of the desk, gazing at his phone.

He looked up, his focus zeroing in like a riflescope. "Nothing else has happened to Hannah, has it?"

"No thanks to us. We're screwing up. Big time. We have to do better and stop this guy from getting to her again. I can't..." Raw emotions raged through his body. He clamped his mouth closed and ran a hand through his hair while trying to gain control, but Ellwood's picture kept flashing in his brain like a warning alarm.

"This guy's proven he has skills," Jackson said. "Military or law enforcement for sure. Best bet is to keep her locked in the house and the team on guard duty twenty-four seven."

Gage glanced at the other team members. "Riley, don't take this the wrong way. I mean, I value your law enforcement experience and training, but her attacker moved with a finesse and confidence I've only seen in spec ops."

"No offense taken," Riley replied. "I saw the hide he took the shot from. No one makes a shot like that without elite sniper training. If the deer hadn't bounded onto the road, that bullet would've been right on target, and she'd be dead."

A gasp came from the doorway. Gage spun to see Hannah standing at the threshold, her hand clutched over her mouth.

Talk about bad timing. In her emotional state, hearing Riley's comment was the last thing she needed. Still, it was probably good for her to recognize she faced a worthy adversary and realize she had to be even more vigilant.

She took a step back, and he thought to take her hand, but didn't want to raise questions with the team, and he'd just promised himself to think of her as a client.

"We're upping our security measures, and you'll be safe here. I promise." He had no business making such a promise. Sure, he could do his best, but sometimes things went sideways. It's just...he had to say something to give her hope.

After a clipped nod, she took in a breath and blew it out, her famous resolve firmly back in place. Still, he saw a chink in her armor, and he prayed that she could weather this latest setback.

She handed her phone to Eryn. "I'm sure this is secure, and my GPS isn't on, so I doubt he could be tracking me this way."

"At least not that you know about." Eryn started tapping the smartphone. "You could have clicked on an email or text that installed a tracking app on your phone."

"I know better than to click on strange emails or text links."

"Good deal, but emails can be spoofed to look like they were sent from someone you trust."

"I don't think that happened, but I hope you *do* find something. That way we'll know how he's been following me and can stop him. Maybe we could even set a trap for him."

"What if after you fled the cottage, he put a tracking device in your purse?" Alex asked.

"Mind if I check it out?" Gage held out his hand.

She pulled the canvas bag from her shoulder. "You don't really think you'll find anything, do you?"

He shrugged, not wanting to admit he thought that at this point anything was possible. "I'll be dumping this out on the desk, so if there's anything you don't want us to see..."

"Nothing in there you won't find in any woman's purse."

"Um." Eryn grinned. "I think that's exactly what he means. You know, girlie things."

As understanding dawned, Hannah's face colored. "I'm good with you seeing everything, but will you be?"

Despite the tension in the room, Gage chuckled at her comment and dumped the contents onto his desk.

"Did you leave *anything* at home in Portland?" he joked as he pushed through keys, a small dinosaur, protein bars, hand wipes, sanitizer, Band-Aids, and on and on. He opened a few items, then ran his fingers over the bag itself for a hidden device. He looked up at Hannah. "Nothing."

"Nothing here, either." Eryn set Hannah's phone on the desk.

Gage's cell rang and, when he saw Blake's number, he answered.

"We recovered the missing skull," Blake said.

"Where?"

"Hidden in a hollowed-out tree in the woods close to where the boat was dumped. A pair of teens found it."

"Interesting." Gage's mind raced over the implications of Hannah's attacker discarding the skull.

"The reconstruction is destroyed, but the skull's intact," Blake continued. "I have to believe if Hannah's attacker killed Jane Doe, he would have destroyed the skull to keep Hannah from continuing the reconstruction."

"Sounds like you think her attack has nothing to do with the skull and is someone like Ellwood," Gage said, drawing everyone's attention, but it was the way Hannah lurched back that hit Gage like a punch.

"Yeah," Blake replied. "We're dealing with another motive here."

"But what?"

"No idea, and if it's not Ellwood targeting her, I have to warn you. We're fresh out of leads, and it'll be nearly impossible to find the guy before he strikes again."

The team exited the office, leaving Hannah alone with Gage. She couldn't seem to catch a full breath. She wrapped her arms around her stomach. Tried to calm herself. But how could she when they suspected the attacks didn't have anything to do with Jane Doe and someone was specifically targeting her?

Her! The most basic, *live your life as good as you can and mind your own business* kind of person, targeted for murder. Murder—for goodness' sake! She could hardly process it.

She took a deep breath but got little air. Her throat closed. Her chest convulsed.

Maybe she should pray. *Odd.* She hadn't considering doing so for eons, but she had to remain levelheaded. She was the key to finding this man now.

"You need to sit." Gage took her by the shoulders and settled her in a chair. He knelt in front of her and took her hands in his. "Just breathe, honey. Slow, deep breaths. Like this."

He drew in a long breath. Let it out. She mimicked his actions. Over and over until the air filled and expanded her lungs.

"Better?" he asked.

She nodded and continued the breathing pattern until the tightness in her chest completely eased.

Her phone rang from the desk. Gage stood and glanced at the screen.

"It's the Deschutes County Sheriff's Department."

Her heart lurched.

"A job maybe?" He handed it to her.

"I've never worked with them, but Nick fell at Smith Rock State Park in their county and they investigated. It must be about him." She accepted the call and tried to hide her unease.

"Ms. Perry," the male said. "This is Deputy Warner from the Deschutes County Sheriff's Department. If you remember, I'm the one who investigated your husband's fall. We had a witness come forward a few days ago, and she's shedding new light on his fall."

"A witness? Really? Someone saw Nick that day?" Stunned, Hannah stared ahead, connecting with Gage's wide-eyed interest. She couldn't concentrate with him watching. She got up and walked to the window to put her back to him.

"Her name is Elyse Ramos. Do you know her?"

"No, but why didn't she report this when he fell?"

"She didn't know about the accident."

"But if she's a witness, how's that even possible?"

"She's from Mexico and was vacationing with family that week. She'd gone hiking and ran into Nick on a trail, but she left that afternoon to return home and didn't hear the news stories about his fall. She came back this week to visit family again, and when she went to Smith Rock, another hiker told her about Nick."

"What did she have to say about seeing him?"

"He wasn't alone. He was with another climber."

"Not alone?" Hannah's heart thudded in her chest.

"No, and it's highly suspicious that the other climber took off instead of reporting Nick's fall."

Hannah managed to stifle her gasp of surprise. "You think he might have pushed Nick?"

"It's a possibility."

Could it be true that Nick hadn't fallen? That someone had murdered him?

She widened her stance to ground herself as she felt as if she was in some alternate world where everything she knew had turned upside down. "I don't suppose after two years she remembers what this other man looks like."

"Actually, she does. Apparently he's quite handsome and a real flirt. She said she'd never forget his face. She also said he had a tattoo on his forearm matching Nick's."

"Nick's was a SEAL trident." Were they teammates? Brothers in arms and the other guy killed Nick?

Could this really be true? The muscles in her legs seemed to liquefy. She hurried back to the chair before they gave out.

Gage cast a questioning look her way, but all she could think of was asking him to hold her as he'd done earlier and tell her yet again that everything would be okay. She turned her attention back to the call. "Do you think this woman is telling the truth? I mean you interviewed so many people who were in the park that day and none of them saw this other man with Nick."

"Her story seems legit, and I'm reopening the investigation. If this other guy really did push Nick, he could have planned it in advance and met up with him on a trail in hopes no one would see them together."

"Then why flirt with Elyse and draw attention to himself?"

"Maybe he hoped he'd leave her too flustered to remember details."

"Sounds possible, I suppose." Did it? Did it really? She didn't know. "How will you proceed?"

"We're looking for a forensic artist to meet with Elyse and draw a sketch of this guy. But, as you know, there aren't many artists in the area, and it could take time before we can get on someone's schedule."

"I'll do the sketch," she said before thinking about it. "And I won't charge a penny, so your sheriff should be happy about that."

"I wouldn't think of asking you. Not with your personal connection to the case."

"I'm doing it. End of discussion. If Nick was murdered, there is no one who wants to find his killer more than I do."

~

Gage gaped at Hannah. He could hardly believe a witness had come forward now when Hannah was dealing with a death threat. He felt for her and didn't care if he was thinking of her as a woman instead of a client. He wanted to ease her pain, but more importantly, he had to focus on her safety. He wasn't about to let her run off to Bend to draw this man's sketch when a stealthy killer was after her.

"You can't go." He reached out to take her arm—as if holding on would prevent her from leaving.

She stepped back. "It's not up to you."

"But your life is still in danger, and I won't allow you to put yourself in a vulnerable position." He planted his feet wide as if he could physically keep her here. "You have to drive over the Cascades to get to Bend, and you'd be a sitting duck on the mountain roads."

She crossed her arms and held his gaze. "Nick was my husband, and now that it looks like he was pushed, I have to help. You would do it for Cass, right?"

His jaw clenched, but he reluctantly nodded.

"Besides, if Nick *was* murdered, maybe the same person is my attacker. If the deputy finds this guy, it could end my problems, too."

Gage had been too busy worrying about her safety to consider the possibility of a connection. "You think Ellwood's not our guy and this could be the man who attacked you?"

"It's as likely as anything else."

"But why now? Why *two years* after Nick died?"

"Maybe because the woman came forward."

"But there's no concrete connection, right?"

"Just that the hiker had a trident tattoo on his forearm like Nick, and we think the guy after me is—or was—spec ops."

Gage thought about her comment and had to agree that

the man sneaking into the compound the other night could easily have been a SEAL. But Gage didn't want to believe a fellow SEAL was capable of committing murder. Sure, they all knew how to kill, but not an innocent person, much less one of their own. He'd much rather believe it was Ellwood.

But he had to consider all possibilities. "Say this *is* related to Nick's death or Ellwood. Either way, leaving the compound puts you in too much danger."

"Like I said, I have to do the sketch so Warner can locate this man, and we can all go back to our normal lives."

Normal? Normal meant she would go home. Leave him. The thought felt like a knife to the gut, but he wouldn't linger on this topic now and cloud the real issue. "Someone else can do the drawing."

"Not on a timely basis. There are less than forty full-time forensic sketch artists employed in agencies across the entire country. Only one in Oregon that I know of. It could take weeks to get someone for the job. And what if Elyse has to go back to Mexico before then?"

"Then they can bring her to you."

Hannah shook her head. "For the process to work best, she needs to be relaxed. What kind of impact do you think this crazy secure compound will have on her?"

"We'll explain that this man is trying to kill you."

"And then she'll worry he's trying to kill her, too. Again, not a good thing." She planted her hands on her hips. "No matter what you say, I'm going. But... I can't take David. I'd like to leave him here."

"That goes without saying. I won't let a child go headfirst into danger." He scowled at her, hoping it would change her mind, but she tightened her arms and tilted her head in a stubborn stance. If she wasn't directing it at Gage, he'd find it adorable. No way he was letting this woman who had somehow wormed her way into his heart step into danger alone. "I'm going with you. I don't care what you say about that, but—"

She held up her hand. "No need to plead your case. I was hoping you'd offer to accompany me."

"Well...good...good." He blinked, caught totally off guard.

She smiled at him. A soft, warm smile that melted his concern and replaced it with awareness of her as a woman. Her curves. Her silky skin. Her full lips, soft and ready for kissing. He knew the feeling. The touch. Years ago. He wanted it now. Again. Couldn't have it.

He forced himself to look away. "I'll get to work researching the area and plan a safe route."

He charged out of the room to head outside for a breath of air. The total darkness evaporated her smile from his mind, and the cold light of danger settled in.

He'd stay by her side, every second of the trip, that was for sure. He'd leave a team behind to protect David, have a forward team scout the trip, and a team bring up the rear. He'd pull out all stops to protect her—the woman he loved.

There, he admitted it. He was in love with Hannah again. No way he'd screw things up and lose her a second time.

10

The helicopter touched down at the Bend Municipal Airport, landing within the white circle painted on the asphalt, the hot afternoon sun radiating off the tarmac. The jarring bump raked along Hannah's nerves, and her pulse raced. She'd been brave with Gage last night. But now? Now she could barely contain her fear of stepping out of the chopper where another bullet could come whizzing through the air and end her life.

"Stay here." Gage leveled a warning look in her direction, then opened the door and jumped down. Coop shut down the chopper and joined Gage.

They both shielded their eyes from the sun and made a full circle over the unprotected area holding two other helicopters neatly nestled in round circles. Gage said something to Coop, who came back to the helicopter to grab their bags, including Hannah's hand-held easel she'd designed for her work. Thankfully, she'd stored it in her car and didn't have to travel to Portland to get it or improvise with something makeshift. The right tools at hand would help her be more at ease when she met with Elyse.

Coop toted their luggage across the tarmac to the hangar

while Gage stood guard at the door. He widened his stance, his hand drifting to his sidearm and settling in place. She totally and completely trusted Gage to do his best to make sure she remained safe.

Her phone signaled a text. She glanced at it to find a message from Eryn with a picture of David and the new orange cast he'd received before Hannah had left Cold Harbor. The message read, *David wanted me to send you a picture so you didn't forget about his awesome cast.*

Hannah smiled at his proud expression as he displayed the neon-colored cast already signed by Gage's entire team. How she wished she were there with him, but Eryn and Opal would take good care of him as she helped find his father's killer.

Coop returned and took over guard duty, his protective stance mimicking Gage's wide-legged posture. What an amazing team she had on her side. It hit her then. Right between the eyes. She hadn't been able to understand why God had put her in this situation, but now she agreed with Gage. God had arranged for this amazing man to protect her. Maybe God had been looking out for her all along, and when Nick died, she'd become blind to His presence.

She felt Him nearby now. His comfort. Even His love. Two years of wandering in the wilderness alone without God at her side had taken a toll. Now she wasn't alone any more.

Thank You, Father. I'm so sorry for my doubt.

Gage approached the helicopter door. "We go straight to the hangar. No dallying. Stay by my side. Got it?"

She nodded and stepped to the door, her heart lighter. Gage took her hand to help her down and the shock of his touch had her pausing for a moment. When he eyed her, questions alive and pressing in his expression, she jumped down and quickly extricated her hand. He apparently hadn't seen how his touch flustered her, as he put an arm around her waist and pulled her tight against his body. His other hand rested on his sidearm. She was snug and safe. Gage and God had her in their hands, what more could she ask for?

She mentally shook herself. She needed to keep her feelings at bay, as she still wasn't ready for another relationship. Might never be. It wouldn't be right to lead Gage on. She resolved to do her best to keep him at arm's length and make sure Coop was with them as much as possible. She looked up at him, but he remained standing at the helicopter.

"Coop isn't coming with us?" Her voice rose, giving away her dismay.

"Can't risk sabotage to the chopper, so he'll head straight back."

What? No. "But we could be here for several days."

"And your point is?"

"We'll be alone."

"And?"

"And you know that's not a good idea."

"I'm not a schoolboy, Hannah." His voice vibrated with frustration. "No matter how attractive I find you, I can control myself."

"No, I... I didn't mean you couldn't. I just—sorry!" Her face burned.

He gave a clipped nod, but he kept his gaze roving over the area, so she couldn't tell if he was mad or simply focused on protecting her.

In the hangar, she pushed free. His eyes tightened, but he said nothing until they reached the door to the parking lot. "I have a buddy waiting with a car. Same drill as at the chopper. Straight to the car."

They hurried to an SUV where a redheaded man with

startling blue eyes stood watching. His posture rigid, he wore a khaki uniform that molded to a very fit body. Hannah knew she'd met him before but couldn't remember where. Gage ushered her into the backseat, not giving her a chance to figure it out. He slid in beside her while the man slipped behind the wheel.

"You and Trey met before, right?" Gage asked. "Back when we were together, he stayed with me for a weekend."

"Right," she said, the weekend coming to mind when the two of them were inseparable. "You're a Green Beret."

"Was a Beret," Trey said. "Now a Deschutes County Deputy."

"Thank you for helping out, Trey."

"No problem." He smiled at her in the rearview mirror.

She expected they'd drive straight to the sheriff's office, but Trey headed away from the city and took a route over arid land dotted with sagebrush. Oregon's high-desert area always amazed Hannah with its direct contrast to the rainy Willamette Valley and coastal regions of the state.

He soon turned down a long drive lined with bitterbrush and tall junipers. The clearing held a two-story home with rough-hewn siding and elaborate stonework. A patrol car sat in the brick driveway.

"I thought you might want to freshen up before going to the office," Gage said. "But let us scope things out first. I'll be right back." He hopped out, not giving her a chance to argue.

Not that she wanted to. It would be good to clean up before meeting Elyse.

The men made a cautious search of the area, Gage remaining in eyesight at all times, and finally Trey retrieved their bags. Gage escorted her to the door, and the sound of running water came from behind the contemporary house.

Through large windows, she discovered that the home looked out over the Deschutes River.

Gage fit a key in the lock. "Trey's uncle owns the place. That's Trey's patrol car, and he's headed to work."

They'd be alone. Here in a secluded house. Together. The two of them. *No.* She wouldn't think about that. She'd keep her focus on Elyse and on finding Nick's killer, if indeed someone had pushed him off that cliff.

Inside, she took her tote bag from Gage. "I'll find a bathroom and clean up so we can get going."

Down the hall she found a lovely yellow bedroom with attached bath, and she made quick work of washing up, all the while hoping that Elyse would be able to communicate her thoughts in a succinct manner and the sketch would proceed smoothly. Maybe they could return home tonight.

Home, right. Go back to Gage's compound. His world. Despite the security and fortress-like atmosphere, it was becoming a place where she was starting to feel comfortable. Was she really falling for him again, or was she simply grateful for his care and attention? Once they apprehended her attacker, would the emotions fade?

"Grrr. Stop. Just *stop* with the thoughts. You have an important job to do." She flipped her hair over her shoulders and marched to the family room.

The drive to the sheriff's office was uneventful, and after a quick talk with Detective Warner, she settled in a small conference room with Elyse. A sturdily built woman with thick dark hair, she curled her hands in her lap and stared at Hannah. She badly wanted to ask Elyse about Nick to glean any bit of information about her husband's last hours. She wouldn't though. Telling Elyse that she was married to Nick would taint the interaction. She needed Elyse to focus solely on Nick and the other man.

Hannah got out her easel, consisting of a few boards

hinged together with fittings to hold paper, photographs, and other aids she might need in her work. She took out a sheet of vellum-finish watercolor paper and clipped it to the board. After locating a graphite pencil in her bag, she sat and met Elyse's wary gaze.

"Relax." Hannah smiled. "Pretend we're good friends and you're describing this handsome man you met."

Eyes still guarded, Elyse nodded and looked off into the distance. "He had this look—a kind of smile—that said he had a secret. I thought he was just coming on to me because he was such a big flirt. But now I wonder if even then he was planning to kill the other guy."

"We can't think about that, Elyse," Hannah said as a vision of a man pushing Nick over the cliff flashed in her mind, and her heart started pounding.

Maybe the deputy was right. Maybe she shouldn't have taken on this drawing. Well, too late now. She'd have to make the best of it. "Can you give me specifics?"

Elyse met Hannah's question with a blank stare. Not unusual. She took out her copy of FBI's Facial Identification Catalog from her bag and flipped to the base images to show Elyse. "Can you choose the image that fits the basic shape of his face?"

She took the book and examined each page carefully. She finally pointed to a white male with a square, wide face then looked up. "He looked like this, but his face was straighter down to his jaw. And his chin was not so wide."

"Good. Good." Hannah drew a rough outline and showed it to Elyse.

Her forehead furrowed. "Umm, sort of, but his nose was wider. And big, but it fit his face, you know? It didn't seem out of place. And his forehead was higher."

Hannah made the adjustments, and the image sparked Elyse into tossing out additional suggestions, but she struggled with communicating the differences. It felt like pulling an elephant through a funnel to get each little detail right, but they kept at it. As the sun dropped toward the horizon, Hannah held out the sketch one last time for the day, praying it was right and she could head back to Cold Harbor.

"It's him," Elyse cried out. "The guy. Perfect."

Exhausted, Hannah stared at the face of her husband's potential killer. She didn't recognize the man, and as she gazed at his handsome features, she felt nothing other than fatigue. She stood. "I'll give this sketch to Deputy Warner, and then he'll come in to let you know what's next. Thank you for taking a whole day out of your vacation to get this done."

"You're the one who should be thanked," she said. "You spent all day with me when I wasn't much help. And you drew him perfectly. I don't know how you did it, but you did."

Before Hannah melted into a puddle of exhaustion, she exited the room. She found Gage pacing the hallway, Deputy Warner leaning against the wall.

"Good." Warner pushed off the wall. "We were going to give you five more minutes before ending your marathon session for the day."

"We finished." Hannah removed the sketch from the clips.

"Do you recognize the man?" Warner asked.

"No," she couldn't hide her disappointment. She handed the drawing to Warner.

Gage joined them to look over the deputy's shoulder. Gage's head shot up, fierce anger radiating from his eyes as he met her gaze and locked on.

"It doesn't matter if you don't know him." The words came out through Gage's clenched teeth. "Because I do."

11

"Sigmund Daniels," Gage said, his gut churning as the three of them settled into a small conference room. "I have no idea if Sig is still in the service or not, but last I heard he was a recruiter."

Hannah peered at him from across the table. "I heard Nick mention that name once when he was hanging with his teammates. I don't remember why they were talking about him, though."

"You sure it was Sigmund?" Warner asked from his spot at the end of the table.

She nodded. "Hard to forget a name like Sigmund. But some of the guys called him Sig."

"Most of us did when he was on the SEAL teams," Gage said. "I lost touch with him when he was injured and took modified duty as a recruiter."

Warner frowned. "So the guy clearly knew Nick. The question is—is he a killer?"

"And is he the guy who attacked me?" Hannah added.

Gage didn't want to jump to conclusions, but this looked like a solid lead. "He fits the suspect we're looking for. Right physical build. Has the skills to break into a cottage without making a sound and evade my men at the compound. Even track Hannah without being seen. And here's the kicker...he took shrapnel to the leg."

Hannah sat forward. "He has a limp."

"Sometimes, yeah. He had good days and bad days. On the bad ones it was very pronounced."

"We need to find him," Warner said. "Hannah's sketch is good, but now that we know his identity, a photograph would be better for issuing an alert."

"Odds aren't good that we'll find one easily," Gage said. "As a former SEAL he'll be camera shy, and it's doubtful you'll find any public photos."

"I'll request his service records then," Warner offered.

Gage shook his head. "That'll take too long. I can contact my tech person. I'm sure she'll find one faster than that."

Warner frowned. "And I suspect she won't be working through channels I want to know about."

Gage grinned. "Likely not."

Warner pushed to his feet. "Better I don't know about it. I'll leave you alone to contact her. When you have the photo, I'll issue an alert."

Gage wasted no time, but dialed Eryn and put her on speakerphone, allowing Hannah to listen in. He explained the situation. "I need Sig's picture ASAP."

"Shouldn't be a problem. Anything else?"

"Yeah. How long would it take to find out if Sig's still in the navy?"

"I can get that info in a flash if you want to hold on."

"Sure." Gage sat back and glanced at Hannah to see how she was handling the latest revelation.

"Did you know this Sig guy very well?" she asked.

"He wasn't on my team, so not real well, but we trained together. He seemed like an okay guy."

"Then you don't think he's a killer?"

"If only that was true. He has the skills and training to end a life. And sometimes the rigors of war make men lose the appreciation for life and killing is easier."

"Okay, got what you need." Eryn's voice came over the phone. "He left the navy three years ago, and get this—he's in prison for aggravated assault. Nearly killed a guy in a barroom brawl."

"When exactly did this happen?"

Eryn rattled off a date.

"That's the week after Nick died." Hannah shot a look at Gage. "Means he's been in prison since then and can't be the guy who attacked me."

"Not unless he got out," Gage said. "Eryn, did you confirm he was still incarcerated?"

"No. Let me check on it and get back to you." Eryn disconnected.

Hannah sighed. "Now what?"

Gage glanced at his watch. "It's too late to get Coop out here tonight. We'll grab dinner at a local takeout and then head back to the house to eat."

After a quick stop at the detective's desk to say their goodbyes, Gage escorted Hannah to the car, and looked for Sig in the shadows. Not that Gage would spot him if he was there. Stalking was a big part of SEAL training, and he knew how to conceal himself.

Gage quickly picked up a dinner of grilled fish and vegetables, and after searching the house to make sure they were secure, he sat with Hannah at the table on a deck overlooking the river. A cool breeze. The trickle of running water. An owl hooting in the distance. A perfect setting for them to relax, but the night air was drenched with tension.

Life had once been easy with them. Once. Way back then, but not tonight. Still, he kept up the conversation by discussing the weather and the flight back home in the morning. Her replies were only one or two words. Okay, fine. She didn't want to talk. But he did and he wouldn't give up. He continued talking for the rest of the meal.

He pushed back from the table. "Want to sit out here a bit longer?"

She seemed to weigh the question, then nodded. They moved to reclining lounge chairs. Settling in place, he felt the remaining tension as black as the darkness, and he couldn't stand it any longer.

He faced her. "You okay?"

She didn't respond and didn't look at him.

"Are you thinking of Nick?"

She sighed heavily. "Yes, Nick... Regrets... David..."

Gage didn't know how to help her, but he had to try. "I wish I could make things better for you, but all I know to do is catch the killer. On that front, I'm doing everything I can."

She turned and looked at him. "I know you are." Her voice was soft. "I appreciate it. All of it—everything you've done for me."

He nodded and held her gaze.

"We used to be so comfortable together," he said, hoping now that she responded to him they could talk through their past.

"We did." She stared off in the distance.

He continued to watch her, the moon breaking free and casting a soft glow on her face. "I know you want me to leave you alone, but I can't do that."

"Because you're protecting me."

He swiveled on his chair to face her and hoped to draw her attention, but she didn't look at him. "You know it's more than that."

"I don't want it to be."

He would have backed off, but her tone belied her words.

"Don't you?" He prodded.

No response.

Her unwillingness to look at him and engage in conversation frustrated him, so he slipped over to her chair and sat on the leg rest. That got her attention. Only for a moment.

She gazed over his shoulder. "I should turn in."

"It's only eight o'clock."

"It was an exhausting day."

"Is that all, or are you running away from me?"

She shot him a fiery look. "Like you did?"

Instinct almost had him pulling back, but he wouldn't let her run him off without discussing it. "I deserve that. More. All the anger you can throw at me, and all I can do is apologize for the way I acted back then. I'm not proud of it, and my only excuse is I was young. Immature. Wanted something else."

She narrowed her eyes. "I get that, really I do. If you'd only asked just *once* what I thought about you leaving instead of throwing it out there and shutting down."

He grabbed her hand, a sense of urgency to resolve this once and for all filling his heart. "I couldn't ask. Don't you see? You would have asked me to stay. Tried to work things out. But I wasn't able to commit, and no amount of working on it would have changed my mind."

He waited for her to look at him, but she didn't.

"I loved you, Hannah. Totally loved you. I wouldn't have left if I didn't think it was best for you."

She met his gaze then, her eyes dark and liquid with emotion. Despite knowing better, he scooted closer and reached up to touch her cheek. "You said you forgave me, but have you really? It would be amazing if you have."

She took a long breath. Let it out, her skin whispering against his fingertips, tempting him.

"For years, I imagined the day I would see you again,"

she said, her voice low and throaty. "How I imagined it. You would be so sorry for leaving. You'd say your life had been awful because of it, and you'd beg me to forgive you." She sighed. "Now that the day is here, it's nothing like that. Nothing at all."

"I *am* sorry for leaving. So sorry. The rotten way I handled the breakup was all my fault, and I desperately want your forgiveness."

She sat silently for the longest time, then sighed and met his gaze. "I was partly to blame, too. I should have recognized that you couldn't commit and not have given you that ultimatum... just loved you and took what you could offer. So yes, I accept your apology and forgive you." She leaned her cheek into his hand.

Was that a signal of real forgiveness or simply desire?

He pressed even closer to kiss her but paused and waited for her to push him away. When she didn't, he slid his fingers into her silky hair and drew her close.

"Hannah." Her name came out on a breath.

He lowered his head. Their lips touched, igniting a fire in him that he hadn't felt in years. She moaned and moved closer to lift her arms around his neck. He deepened the kiss and never wanted it to end. Never. The thought shocked him and still he couldn't pull away. He lost all ability to reason and kissed her with abandon. She returned the kiss, firing off even more senses.

His phone chimed in the tone assigned to Eryn, cutting through his brain fog, and yet, it took a few rings before he reluctantly pulled back to answer. "What's up?"

"First, I have info on Sig Daniels. Before he went to prison, he worked as an independent contractor for the NSA."

"*The* NSA—as in the National Security Agency?" Gage asked, his mind now fully alert.

"Yep, as an IT specialist. And before you ask, he got out of prison two weeks ago."

Information technology. Interesting. "So he *could* be our guy."

"Yes."

"You have an address for him?"

"Yeah, but you won't like it. He left the address for a cheap weekly apartment rental in Portland with the prison. But when I called the manager to see if he still lived there, she said he took off for the coast on Monday."

"The day of Hannah's attack." Gage gritted his teeth and couldn't even look at Hannah until he knew what else Eryn had found. "You had something else, too?"

"I think I figured out how the attacker is tracking Hannah. If I'm right, he knows where you are right this minute."

Now? Here?

Gage didn't wait for Eryn to explain but grabbed Hannah's hand and pulled her to her feet. He rushed her inside, away from the windows, flipping off lights as they went. He led her to a windowless media room and settled her in a large recliner.

"What's going on?" Her voice was filled with terror.

Gage stayed by the door to keep his eyes and ears open. "First, Sig has been out of prison for two weeks and headed for the coast three days ago."

Hannah gasped.

"Worse, Eryn thinks he knows where we are." Gage put his phone on speaker. "You're on speaker, Eryn, so you can explain to both of us."

"Right. Hi, Hannah," Eryn said. "When we dumped out your purse I noticed you had a cross on your keychain. Is it still there?"

"Yes." Hannah twisted her fingers together.

"Where did you get it?"

"My church mailed them out to us."

"Are you sure it's from your church?" Eryn asked.

"Yes. I mean, the letter inside was on church stationary. It explained that we were to carry it with us as a reminder to pray for our church's building fund."

"Did you ever hear about anyone else getting one or see anything in the church news?"

"I don't know. It came right before I left for vacation, so I didn't see or talk to anyone from church."

"Get the cross, Gage," Eryn demanded. "Check it out to see if it's solid or if it can be opened."

Gage didn't want to leave Hannah alone, but her purse was on the dining table. "I'll be right back with your keys."

He quickly slipped through the house, searching the inky darkness for any sign of an intruder as he moved. Satisfied they were alone, he grabbed the purse and returned it to Hannah. He closed the door, making sure the sweep at the bottom was fully in place to keep light from seeping into the hallway, and flipped on a small lamp.

She dug out her keys and turned over the cross. She pointed at a narrow slot. Gage knelt beside her to put his phone on the table and opened the Leatherman he carried. A quick pry of a blade, and the cross's back popped off.

He pointed at a minuscule device. "An electronic tracking bug."

Hannah's face paled. "No. No. How?"

"How'd you know it was there, Eryn?" Gage got to his feet.

"Remember that old hoax about key fobs that keeps popping up on Facebook?"

"You mean the one where they were given out to unsuspecting people at gas stations and malls so they could be tracked?"

"That's the one. I saw it again today and remembered the cross. I thought the attacker could have specifically targeted Hannah that way. Looks like I was right."

"How could I have been so dumb?" Hannah asked.

"You trusted the source, and that wasn't dumb," Eryn replied.

Gage headed back to the doorway to switch off the light and stand guard. A whisper of a sound caught Gage's attention. He listened carefully. Heard the barest of sounds. The patio door from the deck easing open.

"Get Trey out here," Gage said in a hushed tone then disconnected the call to extinguish the phone's light.

He rushed to Hannah and grabbed her hand again. "Sig —or someone—is here. We're sitting ducks in this room. We need to move. Now!"

12

Hannah remembered Jackson's training the other day. His skills. The team's intensity. A man like that was coming for her. Now—in this house. Panic almost had her running out of the room. Fleeing from the house.

Gage must have sensed her anxiety as he drew her into his arms. Held her close.

"Don't worry, honey," he whispered. "I've got you. Trust me?"

"Yes," she said and meant it. Not only here and now, but always.

He led her down the hallway and stopped in one of the bedrooms to shrug a backpack on, then doubled back to the stairway leading to the lower level. Hannah listened. Waited. Feared a gunshot to the back, but trusted Gage and crept down the stairs behind him. He didn't turn on a light, but the room was bathed with the same moonlight they'd kissed under. It was romantic then, but now it was deadly. It could give them away and end their lives.

Gage hesitated at the patio door, his hand suspended over the handle. Then he eased it open just far enough for them to squeeze through.

On the stone patio, he signaled that they would take a path to the east. He kept hold of her hand, and at a thick stand of trees, he stepped off the path. He dug in his backpack for goggles and strapped them on.

"Night vision," he whispered and drew his weapon.

He took her hand again and led her into the scrub. They climbed over boulders and moved through knee-high grass, steadily heading down the steep incline toward the river.

At the water, he paused and drew her alongside him. "We'll follow the river for now, but we have to stay undercover."

Hannah thought it odd that Gage was running from their foe instead of staking a claim, but maybe he didn't think his injured arm would allow him to stand and fight a former SEAL. Sig's leg injury probably put him at better odds in close-quarter combat.

Gage suddenly stopped, dropping down behind a large bolder and taking her with him. He tipped his head as if listening. She heard nothing but the rushing water crashing over boulders and racing downstream.

He swiveled and placed his gun in her hands. He'd once taught her how to shoot, so she wasn't uncomfortable holding the weapon. But she didn't like firing one and had to admit she wanted to give it back the moment he was done rummaging through his backpack.

"Stay here," he said in hushed tones as his hand came out of the pack gripping a knife and another gun. "If I'm not back in a few minutes, take off along the river."

"Wait, what? You're leaving me?" Her voice squeaked.

He held a finger to his mouth. "I have to go after Sig. Get the high ground. It's our only hope. Watch your back and fire at anyone who comes near you."

"But what if it's you?"

"If it's me, I'll let you know."

He started to get up. She grabbed his arm. Pulled him close. Kissed him. Hard. "I loved you, too. Back then, I mean, and I could again. Might already."

He flashed a quick smile and settled the goggles over his eyes, then silently disappeared in the shrubs like a whisper in the dark.

~

Hannah admitted that she'd loved him. Gage liked it. Liked it a whole lot. But that was the last place his mind could go right now. In combat, any distraction could end lives, and right now, he was in combat with a very capable opponent.

Gage searched through the foliage lit by his NVGs. In the distance, he spotted Sig. Just the sight of him framed in the lenses sent Gage's stomach cramping hard. Not only because Sig was a traitor to all that was good and true, but also because Gage didn't know if he could take the other man. He may have injured his leg, but he could still hold his own in hand-to-hand combat. Gage's arm left him wanting in that area.

Since Sig was willing to kill Hannah and had likely murdered Nick, the guy wouldn't hesitate to put a slug in Gage if he had the opportunity. Still, Gage had his brains and combat experience. He was counting on Sig believing that Gage wouldn't fight with Hannah at his side and not expect him to leave her alone. He didn't like leaving her vulnerable, but he knew she'd fire on Sig if she had to.

He moved forward, each step careful and measured to ensure silence. He continued to mark Sig's forward progress and adjust accordingly. Where were those dang sirens when you needed them? Maybe Trey came alone. Then Gage would hear nothing as Trey would arrive in stealth mode and be prepared to do battle. Or maybe he was on the other side of the county and it was simply taking time to get here.

Gage climbed higher, moving beyond Sig, and then started back toward Hannah. Sig suddenly stopped. Gage followed suit and dropped to the ground. Sig ran his gaze over the area then shook his head and continued. As Gage started to get up, he saw a single blade of tall grass move. Gage lifted his gun. Waited. A hand eased out of the brush holding a deputies' badge. Trey! He was letting Gage know he was there.

Gage lowered his weapon and Trey belly-crawled forward, inch by inch, until he squatted, his thigh nearly touching Gage.

He gestured at Sig's location, and without a word, they communicated a two-pronged attack. They broke up and set out, converging on Sig from both sides. Gage desperately wanted to take the guy down, but with Trey at his side, it would be foolish not to let the man with full use of both arms engage with Sig. Gage would cover Trey while he attacked and disarmed Sig.

Close enough to see the tat on Sig's arm, Gage gave Trey the signal. Trey started to launch himself into the air, but Sig spun and fired.

Trey went down hard.

No! Gage hurled his body at Sig's back, dislodging his rifle. It went flying. On the ground now, Sig's face in the mud, Gage worked to secure his wrists behind him, but Gage's gimpy arm failed him and Sig broke free. He lurched forward. Dove for his rifle.

Gage rolled and pulled his gun free. "Lay a finger on that rifle, Sig, and I'll plug you."

Sig froze, and Gage wished the guy would go for it so Gage could pay him back for hurting Hannah, but he lay there unmoving.

"Hands behind your back," Trey called out as he limped up to Gage.

"Nice to see you up," Gage said.

"Figured you needed my cuffs." He handed them over. "Go ahead and restrain him. I've got him covered."

Gage snapped the metal bracelets on Sig's wrists and was tempted to land a solid punch in payback for attacking Hannah, but hitting a man while he was down wasn't Gage's style.

Trey dropped down on a stump to press a hand against his bloody leg and requested backup on his radio. Gage ripped off his shirt and balled it up to bear down on Trey's leg. He then took his belt and wrapped it around the shirt to put pressure on the wound but not cut off his circulation like a tourniquet would do. He checked Trey's face to see how he was handling the wound and wasn't surprised to see the former spec op guy not even wincing.

"I could use a guy like you on my team," Gage said.

"If this bullet causes serious damage, I might be looking for a job and will agree to join your ragtag team." Trey chuckled, keeping his focus on Sig.

Gage wasn't offended at the comment, as the team *was* pretty ragtag. "You think you can keep a weapon on Sig so I can go to Hannah?"

"No worries," Trey said. "You gonna hold onto her this time?"

Was he? He'd been certain he didn't want a relationship, but then Hannah burst back into his life and into his heart. Now he knew he wanted nothing less.

"Yeah, man. She's a keeper." Gage took off. After announcing his presence, he slipped through the brush and found her with her back to the rock, her legs pulled up. The gun lay on the ground, her arms around her knees.

He dropped down beside her and took her hands. "We have Sig in custody, but Trey's been shot."

She sat forward. "Is it serious?"

"It's his thigh, and I doubt it's life-threatening, but it's always possible."

"Then we should go to him, right?"

"Right." Gage loved how she always put others before herself. She truly was a keeper.

He helped her up and drew her into his arms. He wasn't risking any more time passing before he told her how he felt. "This situation might be resolved, but I love you, Hannah, and I don't want you to leave Cold Harbor."

She arched a brow and watched him as if she'd forgotten all about her declaration less than an hour ago. Maybe as she waited for his return she'd been thinking the worst and regretted declaring her love for him.

"I'm not running anywhere this time, honey," he said. "I'm here to stay. Forever, if you'll have me."

She gently cupped the side of his face. He waited for her admission of love. For her to say she wanted to be with him, too. She took a deep breath and blew it out. "We can talk about this later. After we're sure Trey's okay."

Gage nodded, but he had to admit it stung that she didn't tell him she loved him right then and there and agree to spend the rest of her life with him. Not only stung but left him worried she'd simply reacted in fear before. Maybe this was a one-way street, and she didn't want to be with him.

Hannah could hardly look at Sig Daniels. She was certain he killed Nick, and standing this close to him made her sick to her stomach. But she wouldn't leave. While they'd waited for backup, Trey suggested in a whispered conversation that she try to get Sig to explain himself and confess to Nick's murder. As much as she hated the smug look on the creep's face, she'd stand her ground and talk to him for Nick's sake.

"Why kill Nick?" she asked bluntly. "What did he do to you?"

"Never said I killed him." Sig scoffed from where he sat on the ground and leaned against a tree trunk. "Besides, if I did—and I'm not saying I did—you know the reason, so quit playing dumb with me."

This guy was obviously crazy. "I have no idea what you're talking about."

"Liar."

"Watch it." Gage lifted his fist, his body shaking with anger. "Or I'll change my mind and you'll feel my wrath."

Sig rolled his eyes. "Like I'm afraid of you any more than I was of Nick."

Gage took a step closer. "Seems like you're afraid of a helpless female or you wouldn't have resorted to attacking Hannah."

Sig growled, low and menacing. "I'm not going back to prison. Ever. And I'll do whatever I need to do to stop her from making that happen."

"But I haven't done anything," Hannah protested. "How many times do I have to tell you that?"

"Stop it. Just stop it." His hot angry eyes fixed on her.

She had to work hard not to shudder and show him that even in cuffs he was scaring her.

"I followed you to the federal prosecutor's office last week," he said. "Then I found the files at your house. I don't know why you waited so long to turn me in, but I couldn't let it happen."

Hannah shot a helpless look at Gage, telling him she still didn't have a clue about what Sig meant. She didn't anything about these files and had only gone to the prosecutor's office because she was doing a sketch for them.

"Gee, thanks for telling me about all of this, Hannah." Gage's bitter look directed at her took her by surprise. He focused on Sig and shook his head. "Women. You commit to protecting them, and then they don't give you all the details."

What? Where was that coming from?

"Ain't that the truth," Sig mumbled. "Sounds like you and me have the same problem."

Oh, right. She got it now. Gage was taking over and trying to get Sig to confess.

"Had enough of it when my wife filed for divorce," Sig continued. "Stupid divorce. Stupid ex. She left me with barely enough money to live on. Had to run up my credit cards just to buy food. Then I couldn't make the credit card payments. Only way out of that mess was to sell a few classified documents."

Documents? Did he mean NSA documents?

"Well, you had to do it," Gage said. "It was your ex's fault. She left you no choice. You had to eat."

"Yeah, man. I only took a few, you know. Just to pay off the cards and get a little breathing room. Nothing big that would rock our national security. Just minor stuff."

"Nick into this stuff, too?"

"Nah, but something in one of his ops seemed hinky to him. So he ran it down and got wind of my deal. He demanded to see me at Smith Rock that day. Told me to turn myself in or else. I wasn't going to prison. No way." He scowled. "Not that I managed to avoid it for other reasons."

He'd stopped short of admitting to killing Nick. Hannah opened her mouth to get him to confess, but a warning look from Gage stayed her words.

"I can feel your pain, man," Gage said. "Hannah lied to

me. She's had me running in circles for the last few days when she knew what this was all about. She's still not willing to spill, but I'll bet you're right."

"I knew it! Knew it all the time. Lying about wanting to turn me in. Holding on to those NSA documents." He glared at her. "But I underestimated you, didn't I? You and those tools you were using to do your creepy work at the cottage? My arm is still aching."

"She deserved it, though, right?" Gage snagged Sig's attention again. "Deserved for you to keep coming after her?"

"You know it." He blew out a long breath. "Man, it's good to talk to someone who understands."

"I understand more than you know. She was once my chick, and Nick stole her from me."

"Then you can thank me for shoving him over the edge." He chuckled. "Too bad you didn't see the surprised look on his face when he fell. Yeah, he thought he was all that. But he wasn't now, was he?"

He admitted to killing Nick so matter-of-factly that Hannah's heart ached. Nick meant nothing to this guy. Less than nothing.

Gage faced Trey. "Is that enough to put this jerk away?"

Trey nodded. "Thanks for doing my job for me and getting his confession."

"Now wait a minute," Sig said. "I didn't confess to anything."

"Nice try." A satisfied smile slid across Trey's face. "We have three witnesses who heard your confession. You won't be seeing the light of day for a very long time."

EPILOGUE

It was Labor Day weekend, and—after a whirlwind of days that could compete with the biggest of tornadoes—Hannah remained in Cold Harbor. She'd told herself she'd stayed to finish Jane Doe's reconstruction, which she'd done. The deceased woman, Mary Holloway, traveled to Texas every winter to stay with family then returned to Oregon for the summer. She'd been hitchhiking when a trucker picked her up, and he now sat in jail charged with murder and was awaiting trial.

Mary would be laid to rest near her family, and Hannah's involvement in the case was over. Yet, she was still here. At Gage's compound. Spending blissful days with him, Mia, and David. Days like today—a lazy, glorious day. Sun shining, bees buzzing. The air a cool sixty-five and the team and Gage's family all gathered for a big barbeque where the men had claimed best grilling rights, including Trey, though he wouldn't be putting any weight on his injured leg.

He'd been discharged from the hospital, but the verdict was out on whether he would suffer permanent damage. Permanent injury or not, Gage had already offered Trey a spot on the team, and Hannah thought he might take him up on it. Not because of the job or even his friendship with Gage, but because of the way Trey gazed at Eryn as if she was the only woman left on earth, and he had to snap her up before another guy had the chance.

It wasn't hard to recognize the look. Gage's face had held the exact expression for the last few days while he waited for her answer about staying in Cold Harbor. She'd tried each day to conjure up the past pain between them. Nothing happened. Nothing at all. She was over their past. Fully over it. Though committing to Gage frightened her—talk about role reversals—she was ready to acknowledge that she wanted to be with him and see where things went from there.

She left David playing with Mia and stepped up to Gage near the grill. "It's time to let one of the guys take over."

"Something wrong?" he asked with a wary bent to his tone.

She twined her fingers with his. "No. Something is very right."

He got a gleam in his eyes and shoved the spatula into Jackson's hand. "Overcook the burgers and you'll pay for it."

Jackson scoffed, but Gage didn't seem to notice. He tugged on her hand and they slipped around the house for privacy. He led her onto the porch to the whitewashed swing. "What's this about?"

"Us."

"Us?" His voice squeaked high, and it tickled her that she had the ability to fluster such an unflappable man.

She slid closer and ran a finger down the side of his jaw, and she thought he might launch himself from the seat. "I've been thinking about your suggestion that I stay in Cold Harbor."

"And?"

"And, I figured I could work from here. I mean, I'd have

to travel, but if you're willing to watch David sometimes, I think I can do it."

"You don't have to work if you don't want to."

"You mean be a kept woman?" she joked, but when he slid from the bench to his knees, all jokes ceased in her mind.

"Not a kept woman. My wife." He smiled up at her, belying a hint of uncertainty lingering in his eyes. "I love you, Hannah. Will you marry me? Marry me and make us a family. Me. You. David and Mia. All together."

"This is so sudden."

"Is it, or is it ten years too late?" He bit down on his lip.

"I...I..." she said, but thoughts of a lifetime with Gage stole her voice.

"*Yes* is all you have to say."

"Yes." The word whispered out.

Gage shot to his feet, lifted her into his arms, and swung her in a circle. "I promise to be the husband you deserve. The father David deserves. And to love you for the rest of our lives."

"I can't ask for anything more than that," she said into his neck.

"Wait." He stopped spinning and set her down. "A ring. You deserve a ring. I'll get one as soon as possible and make this official."

"I don't need a ring to make it official." She smiled up at him. "A kiss will do."

"Oh, right. Yeah. You don't need to ask me twice for that." His head swooped down and their lips connected.

A crash of emotions rolled over her like a tidal wave, and her knees went weak. She curled her arms around his neck and clung to him for dear life.

Why had she waited so long to agree to this? She would

have to be plumb crazy not to want this wonderful, amazing man in her life for good.

"Gage," Opal's voice floated around the corner. "Jackson says he needs you."

Gage lifted his head but held onto Hannah. "Guess we better go see what he needs or we'll have a bunch of hungry guys hunting us down. You don't want to see my team when they're deprived of food."

Opal rounded the corner and stopped dead in her tracks. "Will you look at that! It's about time you two quit mooning over each other and did something about it. I thought I was going to have to knock some sense in the pair of you."

Hannah laughed. "All my fault, Opal. I was dragging my feet."

"But she agreed to marry me. You heard it and now she can't back out."

Opal let out a loud whoop and came running to hug them.

"About Jackson," Gage said as he extracted himself.

"He says the propane's run out. I told him there's a spare tank in the garage, but he said he wants you to hook it up." Opal rolled her eyes.

Gage grabbed Hannah's hand and the three of them set off.

"Keep this to yourself, Opal," he warned. "Until we can tell Mia and David."

"Mark my words, they'll both be over the moon."

Hannah knew David would be thrilled, but she wasn't as certain Mia would respond well. Sure, she'd opened up a bit the last few days, but still, she'd been unpredictable. One minute she seemed to like Hannah. The next minute she was reserved. She rarely accepted a touch or hug...hanging just out of reach.

Gage went into the garage, and Hannah sat at the table where David was gulping down a bottle of water like he'd come from a desert. Gage finished connecting the tank, and after serving the burgers and hot dogs, he came to stand behind Hannah and placed a hand on her shoulder.

Wondering how Mia might react to Gage touching her, Hannah looked for the little girl and spotted her with Gage's parents. She peeked around her grandmother's leg.

"Mia," David shouted. "Come eat with me."

She came running in her precious little gait, but suddenly stopped and eyed Hannah and Gage. Hannah couldn't read the child's expression and could hardly breathe, wondering how she would react. She stopped directly in front of Hannah, her eyes filled with trepidation. Hannah's heart creased, wishing she knew what to do for this little urchin whose brain put her in a muddle of confusion much of the time.

Hannah opened her mouth to speak—to say what, Hannah didn't know—but then Mia took a few more steps and slid up on Hannah's lap. Her back to Hannah, she sat there as if this was the most normal thing in the world. If Hannah had been baffled over what to do before, this was even more perplexing. She glanced at Gage for guidance, his shocked expression speaking volumes.

Mia sat there motionless until Gage stepped around the side of the table and held up a large knife. "Now who wants watermelon?"

His gaze first landed on Mia, then on Hannah, a heart-melting smile beaming from his face.

Mia's hand shot up. "I do, Daddy!"

"Me, too," David said.

And just like that, with the simple promise of watermelon hanging in the air, they all seemed to let out a sigh of relief and morphed into a little family on the brink of a promising future together.

~

Enjoy this book?

Reviews are the most powerful tool to draw attention to my books for new readers. I wish I had the budget of a New York publisher to take out ads and commercials but that's not a reality. I do have something much more powerful and effective than that.

A committed and loyal bunch of readers like you.

If you've enjoyed *Cold Terror*, I would be very grateful if you could leave an honest review on the bookseller's site. It can be as short as you like. Just a few words is all it takes. Thank you very much.

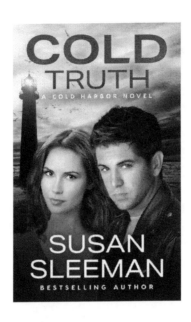

Want to play a game?

When research chemist Kiera Underwood receives a cryptic phone call about her twin brother, she tries to contact him to no avail. Her twin sense tingles, warning her that something is wrong. When he doesn't return her call and his supervisor at Oceanic Labs claims he didn't come into work, she heads to Cold Harbor. But when she arrives in town to find the door to her brother's house ajar, she races to the lab to question his fellow employees.

Solve the puzzle and save your brother...

Kiera's terrified when an attempt is made on her life. Then Blackwell Tactical operative Cooper Ashcroft delivers her second shock of the day. Someone stole a deadly biotoxin. The main suspect? Her brother-and Blackwell Tactical has been hired to bring him in. If that wasn't distressing enough, she's suspected of colluding with him. She had nothing to do with the theft or murder, and despite the evidence staring her in the face, she knows that her brother is innocent of all charges. She sets out to prove it, putting her in the crosshairs of the killer. As Coop tries to protect her as well as solve the crime, he grapples with the possibility she's telling the truth and someone has likely abducted her brother-perhaps killed him. Now Kiera's life is in serious danger and Coop must protect her while discovering the cold truth behind the theft.

~

Chapter One

"Want to play a game?" the scrambled voice rasped through Kiera's phone.

"Who is this?" she asked, irritated that someone would prank call her and use one of those voice-altering devices to do it.

"Solve the puzzle and save your brother."

"What? What puzzle?" She was getting angry now. "And my brother is fine."

"Are you sure?"

"Of course I am. I just talked to him last night. Not that it's any of your business." She sighed. "Who is this anyway?"

"I guess if your brother is fine, you don't need to know." Silence filled the phone for an uncomfortable moment. "Open your mind to my request, Kiera, or your brother will die."

The line went dead. She stared at her phone. This had to be some sort of a joke. A stupid joke, but still, a senseless one.

She pressed redial for the caller. No answer. No voicemail message. Just silence. "Sure, run and hide, but when I find out who you are..."

She punched her twin brother, Kevin's, icon on her phone. It rang. Once. Twice. Continued ringing. Voicemail picked up.

"Kev," she said after the tone. "Call me the minute you get this message."

Other people might panic after getting a call like this and their sibling not answering, but Kevin often failed to answer his phone. He got lost in his work. Day or night, it didn't matter. She understood that to a degree. After all, she was a research chemist, too, but he took his withdrawal from the world to extreme lengths when he was working on something he loved. And right now, he was involved in a big hush-hush project to synthesize a biotoxin carried by seafood, and he hoped to create an antidote. The lab put great pressure on Kevin to succeed, as they could make big bucks on the antidote. Money that would fund all of their other research.

She scrolled down the contact list on her phone and punched the number for Oceanic Labs in Cold Harbor where Kevin was employed. "Kevin Underwood, please."

"I'm sorry, Kevin isn't working today," the polite female voice responded.

Not at work. Really. Now *that* got Kiera's attention and a spark of worry ignited in her brain. He never missed work. Never. "Are you sure?"

"Pretty sure."

"Transfer me to his supervisor, please."

"She's not in either."

"The lab manager then."

"May I tell him who's calling?"

"Kiera Underwood. Kevin's sister."

"One moment, please."

Kiera got up and started pacing across her living room. Back and forth she moved over the smooth wood floors gleaming in the sunlight pouring through her window. She glanced at her watch. Ten-thirty. She'd had a dentist appointment this morning, or she'd be at work by now. The hygienist had made a mess of her blouse, and Kiera popped home to change. Good thing she'd stopped by. With a call like this, she wouldn't be able to concentrate at work, and that could be deadly in her research for a pharmaceutical lab.

"C'mon, pick up the call already," she muttered under her breath as she stared out the window of her high-rise apartment in downtown Portland.

If the manager didn't know where Kevin was and why he hadn't come to work, she needed to come up with a plan of action. She could call his local sheriff's department, she supposed, but with nothing to tell them other than her brother hadn't gone to work and wasn't answering his phone, they'd dismiss her.

So what could she do other than drive to Cold Harbor and check out his house? Nothing. She'd have to make that five-hour drive to the southern Oregon coast.

"Ms. Underwood, this is lab manager, Nigel Moody. How can I help you?" He sounded helpful, but his tone was restrained.

"I'm trying to locate my brother. The receptionist said he didn't come to work, and he's not answering his phone."

"We'd like to know where he is, too."

"He didn't call off work?"

"No."

"Do you know why?"

"I have my suspicions, but I'm not at liberty to share that with you."

Her spark of worry burst into a full-blown flame, and

Kiera resumed pacing. "Do you think something's wrong with him?"

"Yes. Yes, I do. Something very wrong."

"What do you mean?" Kiera's worry reached full blaze.

Nigel sighed. "Like I said, I can't give you any information, but if you talk to him, be sure he calls me."

"But you have to help me. You just have to." She waited for a response to her plea.

Nothing.

"Hello. Are you there?" She held her phone out. The call had ended. He'd ended the call.

What in the world is going on?

She dialed Kevin again, and when he didn't answer, she ran to her bedroom to pack an overnight bag. She made quick work of it and phoned him again as she started for her front door.

Still no answer.

She exited her apartment and ran for her car in the parking structure. On the way, she called her work to tell them she had a family emergency. She settled her phone in the car's dashboard holder and wasn't surprised to see her hands trembling. Not with her twin missing.

It took all of her concentration to get her car safely on the road and pointed toward Cold Harbor, but once she left the city behind, she dialed Kevin again. Recent legislation now made it illegal to use her cell in Oregon while driving, but her brother's life could be at stake, so she'd risk using it on speaker while it sat in the holder.

The call went to voicemail, and her hope died. "Kev, please. Please call me. I'm worried about you."

As the miles rolled under her car, she replayed the garbled phone call in her brain. Why did this person—a man by the sound of things—want to play a game? A game involving Kevin. A game of life or death. Could this be some sick joke or was Kevin actually in trouble?

She dialed him again. Got his voicemail. She wouldn't give up. She punched his icon every fifteen minutes during the long drive to Cold Harbor. Usually she loved pulling into the small oceanside town. Loved hearing the waves crashing against a craggy shoreline. Loved the smell of the salty ocean air. But today she couldn't get down the beach road fast enough to arrive at his small bungalow.

She raced across the sandy lot and up the stairs. She lifted her hand to pound on the door. Found it open.

No. No. God, no. Don't let this be real.

She wrapped her hand around the mace she carried in her purse and entered. Her fear of finding her brother lying on the floor from some altercation nearly stole her last breath. She flipped on the overhead light and searched the room. His traditional sofa held no pillows or any other item. The set of three matching tables had no décor save a lone lamp. No dust. Not a speck. The usual immaculate place.

"Kev?" she stepped forward. "Are you here?"

No response.

Her pulse pounded in her ears as she made her way to the small kitchen. Then the bedroom he used for an office. She desperately hoped to find him, face in the computer, working on something, and he'd simply not heard her.

His chair was empty and computer off. His desk clear of all objects.

Her anxiety ratcheted up and her legs felt weak, but she continued down the hall to his bedroom. He'd made his bed —not a crease in it, but no Kevin. "The garage."

She raced back down the hallway and jerked open the door. His car sat on the far side of the two-stall garage. She hurried to the small Prius hybrid. Empty. She popped the trunk and headed toward it. Held her breath and looked inside. Just his fishing equipment.

"Where are you?" she cried out in panic and shot a look around the garage trying to figure out what to do next.

She dialed his phone. Waited, prayed for an answer. None.

She glanced at the clock. Almost six o'clock. The lab had already closed. She couldn't call. She'd have to go there and hope he'd shown up.

She pulled the door closed behind her and locked it with the key he'd given her. She sped across town and pulled up to the lab secured with an impenetrable gate. *No. No.* She'd forgotten. She couldn't get into the parking lot. The lab had few visitors, meaning no guest entrance.

Parking on the side street, her mind raced for a way to get through that gate. She spotted a car heading for the exit. She could question the driver. She ran to the driveway and stood in the middle of the road, waving her arms and signaling for the driver to lower the window. The thirty-something blond woman complied, an uneasy look on her face.

"I'm Kevin Underwood's sister," Kiera said quickly. "Do you know him?"

The woman's apprehension faded. "Yeah, sure. He works on the second floor."

"Did you see him today?"

She cocked her head as if Kiera was asking a difficult question. "No. I heard something's going on up on his floor and no one is working up there today."

"You're sure he didn't come in? Not at all?"

"I didn't see him, but then things were kind of chaotic today."

"Do you know what's going on?"

"No, but I heard rumors that it involved the police. Can't

imagine what kind of crime could've occurred here, but the management is keeping it quiet. But I do have to say the way some of the guys dress up there should be against the law." She chuckled.

Kiera couldn't even work up a hint of a smile. Not with Kevin missing and her hope of finding him disappearing with the sun sinking below the horizon.

"Look, I gotta get going," the woman said.

"Will you call me if you hear from him or see him?" Kiera held out her business card.

"Sure, but I doubt I will." She took the card and studied it before looking up, her face tight with concern. "Sounds like you think something bad's happened to him."

"He never takes off work. Never. His car is at his place and he's not answering his phone. I don't know where he is." Kiera's panic inched higher.

"I promise I'll let you know if I see him." She gave a tight smile. "I'm sure it's nothing, and he'll turn up."

Nothing. Right. No way.

Kiera watched the car move down the road and disappear into the dusky night. She stood waiting for the next vehicle. Damp winds rolled in from the ocean, the fishy smell strong. She rubbed her arms for warmth, but the salty air had settled into her lightweight jacket the moment she'd stepped from her car, and she shivered.

Another car approached, and she went into questioning mode. The man hadn't seen Kevin either, so she stepped back and watched his car disappear down the road. She waited for the next car, time ticking away. Thirty minutes passed, and no one came out. She was too cold to remain standing there. She'd go back to Kevin's place and regroup.

She started across the street to her car. Headlights gleamed from the main road, heading toward the lab, the vehicle's engine sounding more like a motorcycle than a car.

Odd. The road dead-ended at the lab. Maybe this person was coming in to work. A person she could question, maybe who would allow her access. She remained in place and would wait for the vehicle to slow at the gate before approaching.

Instead of slowing, the motor revved, and the vehicle picked up speed. It swerved from the path to the gate and headed straight for her.

Headlights pressed down on her.

Didn't he see her?

He came closer. Closer.

She screamed.

She needed to run, but she couldn't get her feet moving.

Move now! She screamed at herself.

And Coop thought his surveillance detail was going to be boring.

He charged out of the trees and scooped the woman up in his arms. She shrieked and flailed against him, but he held tight and dove for the ditch to dodge the ATV barreling toward her. He landed hard on his shoulder and tried to hold his position, but he rolled and came to rest on top of her. She let out an *unh*, sounding like he'd knocked the wind out of her.

The vehicle swerved. Maybe the driver had gotten distracted or hadn't seen her standing there.

Coop rose up on his arms and waited for the driver to stop and apologize, but he reversed course and charged away from the lab, the roar of his engine disappearing into the cloudy night. Coop had tried to get a good look at the driver and his vehicle, but it was too dark to make out any details.

"Please let me up," the woman demanded in a clipped tone.

Right. Her. He'd been so busy watching the ATV that he forgot he was resting atop the very curvy, very pretty woman he'd been watching for the last hour while she'd approached people leaving the lab.

"Sorry about that." He pushed to his feet and offered her a hand.

She ignored it and stood. She brushed off her clothing. Why, he didn't know. She couldn't possibly see any dirt or leaves in the pale glow of distant streetlights.

Her head shot up. She eyed him and took a sudden step back as if planning to flee. "Who are you anyway?"

Coop held up his hands. "No need to worry about me. I'm not some perv waiting to attack. Name's Cooper Ashcroft, but everyone calls me Coop. I'm on assignment for Blackwell Tactical. Saw the vehicle headed for you and reacted."

The moon broke through the clouds. He could see her face clearly now, and a lovely face it was. Big eyes, deep brown like the stock on his favorite hunting rifle. Petite nose. High cheeks. She also had wavy russet-brown hair falling a few inches below her shoulders and stood a head shorter than Coop.

"Thank you for the rescue." She held his gaze. "Seems like it might not have been necessary since he ended up veering off."

Coop didn't think it was quite that simple. "I tried to take the brunt of the fall, but did I hurt you?"

She shook her head and looked a bit dazed. Not unusual. Someone almost ran her over and a strange male had tackled her. He waited for her to offer her name, but she didn't. Not a problem. Coop had known who she was the moment she'd stepped onto the property. One Kiera Underwood, sister to the missing chemist his team had been hired to find, and a chemist herself. Perhaps one who was involved in the theft of a deadly biotoxin that her brother was believed to have stolen.

"What kind of assignment are you here on?" she finally asked, that wary bent lingering in her tone.

"Sorry. Can't divulge that information." He offered his best charming smile that had always been effective with the opposite sex, but she frowned. "So who would want to run you down?"

She shot a look down the road. "You think that was on purpose?"

"If not, the driver likely would have hung around to make sure you were okay, don't you think?"

"Maybe, or maybe he has a hit-and-run kind of personality. You know, not someone who would take responsibility for his actions." She bit down on her full lower lip, her eyes now darkening with fear.

"Something else you're afraid of, ma'am? Other than that ATV."

She eyed him for a long moment. "My brother. Kevin. I got a call...a horrible call saying something was wrong with him. I searched for him all day. He's missing."

"You received a phone call about your brother?" He made sure to keep his tone casual when he wanted to give her the third degree about the missing chemist.

She watched him again. He'd have no problem getting lost in those eyes for a year or two, but she could be involved in the theft and that made her the last woman on earth that he should connect with.

Her eyes narrowed. "Do you know my brother?"

Coop shook his head. He'd never met the guy, but Coop could spout the background data retrieved by his team the second they'd signed the contract with Oceanic.

Name: Kevin Wilson Underwood II. Middle name came from his father. Kevin was thirty years old. Five-nine, thin with cropped brown hair. Clean shaven and brown eyes. His parents wealthy. Old money from a logging empire and they sat on boards for philanthropic causes. The kind of family Coop couldn't understand. Not when he came from a lower income area of Portland. They weren't just on the other side of the tracks, they were in a whole other world.

Still, it wasn't like her parents got everything they wanted. An older couple, they had to turn to in vitro fertilization. Conceived fraternal twins, Kiera and Kevin. They were born and resided in Portland until they got their PhDs in chemistry from the University of California in Berkley. Kevin moved to Cold Harbor after graduating. Kiera lived in Portland and worked for a pharmaceutical lab.

Her eyebrow arched. "If you don't know Kevin, why are you interested in the call I received?"

"You sounded upset. I believe I can help." He wasn't lying. She did seem upset, and he was quite able to help her find her brother.

She frowned. "You're a stranger. How on earth can you help?"

"My team finds missing people. One of the many services we offer."

"Then I want to hire you," she said decisively.

Right. Like she could hire him. Not when the team had already contracted with the lab to find her brother and recover the toxin, but he wouldn't share this information. That would shut things down right off the bat when he needed to keep the lines of communication open with her. Figure out if she was involved. Like faking this hunt for her brother to throw people off his trail.

Coop forced a smile to his lips. "The best thing is for you

to come out to Blackwell Tactical where we can discuss the options."

Her wary watch turned downright skeptical.

"Don't worry. I'm not making this up to lure you into some out-of-the-way place and have my way with you." He took out his phone and opened the Internet. "Go ahead and look us up. You'll see we're legit."

She tapped on the screen and focused intently, occasionally scrolling down the page to read. "You were being modest. You have quite the operation, including training law enforcement." She handed the phone back to him. "And you're all former military special operations or law enforcement."

"Army Ranger," he replied, as he was proud of his service.

"I guess if anyone can find Kevin, it would be a group of people like you."

"Let me make a quick phone call, and then I'll lead the way to the compound."

She nodded and shivered.

"Why don't you wait in your car where it's warmer," he suggested.

"Good idea." She hurried across the road to a small white Honda, and he had to admit enjoying watching the sway of her hips.

Duty, Coop. Duty. Keep your mind on that.

He dialed Gage Blackwell, owner of Blackwell Tactical. "I need someone to relieve me."

"Can't handle standing a little surveillance duty at your old age?" Gage joked, as Coop was only thirty-one.

"I can handle it just fine. But isn't it more important to bring Kevin Underwood's twin to meet with you so she can hire us?"

"Hire us?" Gage's voice shot up. "Are you crazy? She can't hire us."

"I know that, but she doesn't. Not yet." Coop explained the situation.

"Alex and Riley are still training. Eryn's running computer support for them. I'll get Jackson out there on the double."

"Understood." Coop disconnected his phone and started for Kiera's car. After the call with Gage, Coop couldn't help but think about his fellow teammates.

A year ago, he'd joined three other men and one woman on Gage's team. All of them had suffered serious on-the-job injuries that prohibited them from continuing in their chosen professions. They'd also experienced a sense of hopelessness over the loss of the work they loved, and in a sense, their identity. Then Gage gave them their lives back by allowing them to join a team where they could not only use their skills, but their skills were esteemed.

Coop would do anything for his teammates, including taking a bullet for them and especially so for Gage. That meant doing what was best for their current assignment and bringing Kiera to the compound to question her.

He crossed the road, watching for other wayward vehicles. Not that he thought there would be another attempt on her life tonight. If the speeding ATV even was an attempt to kill her.

When he approached her car, she lowered her window. "Everything okay?"

"We're good to go once my associate arrives."

"Thank you," she said, sincerity flowing through her words. "I'm so glad you were here."

A quick smile flashed across her face, and his heart tripped. Oh, man. Even white teeth revealed at the parting of her lips. High apple cheeks going higher. Sparkling eyes with only a hint of worry at the moment. Yeah, she was a beauty all right.

"My brother is everything to me," she added, her vehemence taking Coop aback. "I'd be lost without him."

Great. Now he felt like a real heel. Here he was suspecting her of colluding with her brother, and she seemed genuinely upset by his absence. Coop would love to give her the benefit of the doubt, believe she really didn't know where Kevin had disappeared to, but he couldn't. Not with a missing toxin, that—if weaponized—could kill millions.

No matter how much the despair in those tantalizing eyes made him want to offer comfort, he had to stick to doing his job at all costs. If that meant grilling her to learn if she was involved, so be it. Lives were depending on him.

Available now at most online booksellers!
For More Details Visit -
www.susansleeman.com/books/cold-truth/

Dear Reader:

Thank you so much for reading COLD TERROR, book one in my Cold Harbor series featuring Blackwell Tactical.

Book 1 - COLD TERROR
Book 2 - COLD TRUTH
Book 3 - COLD FURY
Book 4 - COLD CASE
Book 5 - COLD FEAR
Book 6 - COLD PURSUIT
Book 7 - COLD DAWN

I'd like to invite you to learn more about the books in the series as they release and about my other books by signing up for my newsletter and connecting with me on social media or even sending me a message. I hold monthly give-aways that I'd like to share with you, and I'd love to hear from you. So stop by this page and join in!

www.susansleeman.com/sign-up/

Susan Sleeman

BOOKS IN THE COLD HARBOR SERIES

Blackwell Tactical – this law enforcement training facility and protection services agency is made up of former military and law enforcement heroes whose injuries keep them from the line of duty. When trouble strikes, there's no better team to have on your side, and they would give everything, even their lives, to protect innocents.

For More Details Visit -
www.susansleeman.com/books/cold-harbor/

Want to see more of the Cold Harbor characters in action? Keep reading for a sneak peek of the books in my new Truth Seekers Series where the Cold Harbor characters work side-by-side with the Truth Seekers of the Veritas Center.

THE TRUTH SEEKERS
People are rarely who they seem

A twin who never knew her sister existed, a mother whose child is not her own, a woman whose father is anything but her father. All searching. All seeking. All needing help and hope.

Meet the unsung heroes of the Veritas Center. The Truth Seekers – a team, that includes experts in forensic anthropology, DNA, trace evidence, ballistics, cybercrimes, and toxicology. Committed to restoring hope and families by solving one mystery at a time, none of them are prepared for when the mystery comes calling close to home and threatens to destroy the only life they've known.

For More Details Visit -
www.susansleeman.com/books/truth-seekers/

HOMELAND HEROES SERIES

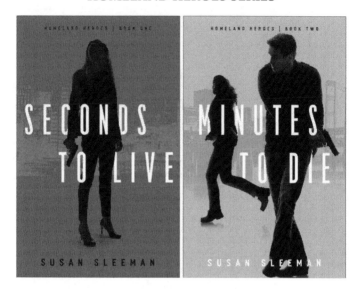

When the clock is ticking on criminal activity conducted on or facilitated by the Internet there is no better team to call other than the RED team, a division of the HSI—Homeland Security's Investigation Unit. RED team includes FBI and DHS Agents, and US Marshal's Service Deputies.

For More Details Visit -

www.susansleeman.com/books/homeland-heroes/

WHITE KNIGHTS SERIES

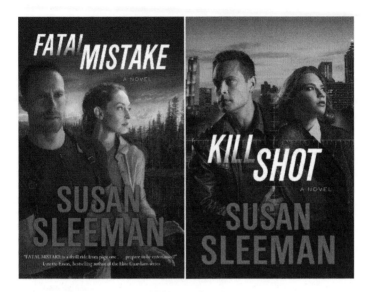

Join the White Knights as they investigate stories plucked from today's news headlines. The FBI Critical Incident Response Team includes experts in crisis management, explosives, ballistics/weapons, negotiating/criminal profiling, cyber crimes, and forensics. All team members are former military and they stand ready to deploy within four hours, anytime and anywhere to mitigate the highest-priority threats facing our nation.

www.susansleeman.com/books/white-knights/

FIRST RESPONDERS

  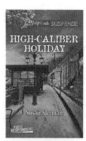

 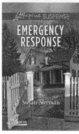 

Join the First Response Squad, a six member county Critical Incident Response team, as they report to explosive emergencies and find themselves embroiled in life threatening situations of their own. And join in on the camaraderie at their home, an old firehouse remodeled to provide a home and team meeting facility for this talented team of law enforcement officers.

For More Details Visit -
www.susansleeman.com/books/first-responders/

MCKADE LAW SERIES

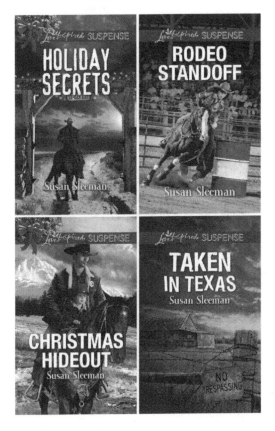

Set in Lost Creek, a fictitious town in the Texas Hill Country, a member of the McKade family has been the county sheriff and/or a deputy for the last 125 years. The series features four McKade siblings along with their grandparents, Jed and Betty McKade, and parents, Walt and Winnie McKade. In addition to law enforcement duties, they also own a working dude ranch. Walt is the soon to retire sheriff, and his children are all law enforcement professionals.

For More Details Visit -
www.susansleeman.com/books/mckade-law/

ABOUT SUSAN

COLD TRUTH - BOOK 2 COLD HARBOR

SUSAN SLEEMAN is a bestselling and award-winning author of more than 35 inspirational/Christian and clean read romantic suspense books. In addition to writing, Susan also hosts the website, TheSuspenseZone.com.

Susan currently lives in Oregon, but has had the pleasure of living in nine states. Her husband is a retired church music director and they have two beautiful daughters, a very special son-in-law, and an adorable grandson.

For more information visit:
www.susansleeman.com

Made in the USA
Middletown, DE
25 February 2022

61828160R00094